# The Raven Who Caught the Canary

## By
## Landra Graf

The Raven Who Caught the Canary
Copyright © 2017 by Landra Graf
ISBN: 978-1-68361-196-7
Cover art by Tibbs Designs

Published by Decadent Publishing Company, LLC
Look for us online at:
www.decadentpublishing.com

# Decadent Publishing Recent Releases

Safe at Home by Wendy Burke

Double Down by Desiree Holt

All I Want by Eden Ashe

Dressing Lily by Siobhan Shannon

One Night in Jersey by Tianna Alexander

Guardian of the Angels by Ashlyn Chase

Sorority Row by TL Reeve and Michele Ryan

The Vessel by Nancy Fraser

Return to Ecstasy by Tina Donahue

## Also by Landra Graf

Raven, Pirate, Assassin, Spy

A Rose by Any Other Name

What You Need

What You Want

What You Crave

What You Desire

# Blurb

Revolutionary and pirate, Luther Corvino, seeks revenge for a lifetime of hell. The German general responsible is the same one building a tunnel to Britain. Kill the man; blow up the tunnel. These tasks should be easy compared to the fights Luther has faced —until he runs into the one woman he's never forgotten. Too bad she'd rather turn him in than play kiss and make up.

Eva Canari has never forgiven Luther for abandoning her in France. Caught for spying, she's been recruited by the Germans as a consort and agent. She'll do anything to get her nightclub, La Roux, back in her possession, even selling out her ex. Trouble is, she's having a hard time betraying him when his touches are sweet heaven, and his charm the devil's own.

Can Luther and Eva rekindle their love, or are they ensnared by a game they may never win?

# Dedication

To Amanda, Lori, and Cate – it takes a village, or in my case three amazing women. From the feedback and brainstorming to the encouragement, I'm thankful for ya every day.

# Chapter One

*New Orleans, 1937*

Some people hated the black market. At the very least, they despised the items sold there. Luther "Sette" Corvino loved what the market stood for. Freedom. Freedom to trade, to deal, and ultimately make whatever decisions a person wanted—if said person had currency to trade in. Otherwise, the people present might find themselves sold versus acquiring.

He ambled through the streets, inhaling the city smells and embracing the yellowed, randomly torn advertisements hanging from the dealers' booths, carts, and stores lining either side. Sure, a lot of merchants sold people, but many encouraged the purchase of weapons, food, and other goods not found in this part of the world, such as silk thread. Yes, he might stop there on the way back, for the thread proved handy for stitches. He'd received plenty of those over the years.

Indeed, the journey to Janken's club, Howl at the Moon, proved to invigorate him, and, by the time he pounded on the front door, his normal foul mood had faded. Then no one answered, and the frown returned, along with his bad habit of grinding his teeth against the head of his cigar. He knocked once more, prolonging the impact of his flesh with wood. The glass pane in the center of the door rattled against the force of his fist.

Finally, the majordomo, the only man in Janken's employ, swiped the red-and-white curtain aside and peeked out at him. Chains slid, locks clicked, and Luther found himself ushered inside.

"I'm here to see your boss."

"He's expecting you. Follow me, sir." The majordomo led him up the red-carpeted stairwell to the left—no main room visit today.

"Is he asleep?"

"No, Captain. He breakfasts."

The privilege of being in this part of the club was not one he'd been granted before. The very concept put him on edge, one hand resting on the hilt of his Bowie knife. In his world, friends were like peace, a false concept. People were easily bought with either currency or information, and, unfortunately, he traveled with only one of the two at the moment.

More elaborately decorated carpet, red with sexual images woven in black through the fabric, passed beneath their boots, and he glanced at depraved pictures and photos lining the walls. Although a blind man, his host cultivated an art collection inspired by his fondness for the tastes of the Marquis De Sade. They finally reached a pair of white double doors, with gold doorknobs. Thick crimson curtains hung on either side, pulled back with wide gold-tasseled ropes—an extra defense to give the impression, when dropped, that a window lay behind them.

The majordomo tapped a simple rhythm out on the door, and the door opened.

"Come in, *mon ami*. Join me in a light repast, eh?" Janken called out to him. He entered, but his feet came to a halt once he got the full view. The albino musician sat at the table, white dreads pulled into a ponytail, dark glasses hiding his useless eyes. A naked ebony-skinned woman lifted her head from his crotch and assumed a prone position on the floor, her heart-shaped bum in plain sight. "You hesitate. You're not against sexual pleasure, are you...like my other American brethren?"

"No." Rather, seeing the woman there brought up memories. Ones he'd rather forget about, earlier years, the years spent serving a madman. "Not at all. Pleasure should be taken when desired. A Cursed core rule." A small lie, since he'd abolished the mercenary rules of the past as soon as he took over five years prior.

"Good. Take a seat, and can I offer you any of my selection?" As the woman resumed her task in his groin, Janken motioned to the right wall, lined by a row of occupied chairs. Not all the whores were of the female gender, and a few girls appeared barely over sixteen. At least they were older than most sold into pleasure services. He'd been much younger.

His internal disgust roared to life, and he tempered it, as he did every time he came to this club. Taking an empty seat on the other side of the table, he replied, "I'll pass. I spent last night with a tasty dish who sought passage from Europe."

The albino picked up his porcelain coffee cup and sipped. "I see. Regardless, they are available if you change your mind. Au lait?"

"Of course." Only a fool turned down coffee, a rarer commodity than even silk thread. The residents of New Orleans made coffee as different as they did everything else. The cultural center, life's blood of the delta region, aspired to provide an environment unlike any other. Coffee with chicory was their specialty, and damn if he hadn't gotten himself addicted to the stuff.

4

Janken snapped his fingers, and a servant came forward, a young man in white tunic and pants. The youth set a cup and saucer on the table, filled it with steaming brew, and hovered his hands over the service.

"Cream or sugar?" his host asked.

"Cream."

The servant poured, glancing at Luther for direction on the correct amount. Luther nodded, and the youth handed him the cup and saucer—so proper and strange at the same time.

"Do you typically employ young men?" He removed his cigar and set the soggy stub next to his saucer before taking a small sip. The drink proved warm, not hot, but still tasted fresh.

"Does it matt—?" Janken's head flew backward as he grunted with his release. The table rattled, and a few drops of Luther's coffee splashed onto the saucer. He tried to look anywhere else, but the sucking and slurping noises permeating the air were hard to ignore. Janken moaned, and when Luther glanced back, the girl had risen and stood beside his host.

"Marie, *mon cher*. You have a gift, and don't let anyone tell you otherwise. Treat yourself to a bath and get dressed." Janken chuckled and patted her on the

5

butt as she sashayed past him. Like nothing happened, the man closed the flaps of his robe, secured it with a tie and scooted his chair up to the table. Another snap of his fingers and servants produced two covered dishes for them, the lids removed seconds after the plates touched the table.

Steam and the scent of eggs and bacon wafted past Luther's nose. Thick-sliced, evenly cooked bacon—not too crunchy or soft. His chef never got it right, either burning the pieces or under-cooking them. These three strips of pork stomach would nearly top his list of most heavenly experiences.

He bit into the first strip and about moaned. For this, he could almost forgive all the other hedonistic things he'd been privy to so far—almost.

"So?"

"The bacon's delicious."

Janken laughed. "I'm not talking about the food."

"If I recall, you sent the message asking me to come here. Therefore, I've come." He dug into the eggs next, the yolks runny the way he liked them. A sprinkle of pepper and they'd—

"General Field Marshal Sauer."

Luther clutched his fork in a death grip. "What about him?"

6

"I discovered where he is, or at least where he will be."

"Impossible. The man's a ghost. I've been trying to find him for years but can never pin him down."

A bite of food disappeared into the albino's mouth, and he finished chewing before speaking. "Yes, I know. But I have an extremely reliable source."

"Where?" His voice betrayed his impatience. *Screw it.*

"France. Not too far from Calais."

A rumor about a large contingent of soldiers moving through Calais had reached his ears, but he'd been unable to verify it. "I'll need more than your word."

"What you want, you have to pay for."

Information for something. Nothing came free in this devious world they lived in. Since the United States denied assistance to the Allied Nations during the First World War, leading to a German victory, everything had turned deceptive and harsh. People starved, desperation took hold across continents, and everyone not touched by the madness held their breath, waiting, hoping for something to end the insanity.

Janken's prices tended to be steeper than others. His accuracy exceeded all competitors, however. Luther reached into his coat pocket and pulled out the small bag. "Not easy to procure something worth your price."

The albino rubbed his hands together, the pasty white skin so unlike Luther's tanned hide. "Yes, but you got them?"

"I did." He untied the strings and pried open the black velvet pouch. A ruby necklace and twin teardrop earrings tumbled out with a thump. Heavy jewelry and heavier trouble as far as Luther was concerned. It had been a challenge to charm these from the prime minister of Spain's wife. All the same a well-placed caress and a few stolen moments in her bedroom earned him the prize, though his escape route had almost been cut off by some idiot who got a little too drunk. Another too-close moment in a lifetime of them, which forced him to be faster and more intelligent than his predecessor.

"If these eyes could see what these hands feel." Janken hoisted his prize and draped the necklace around his neck. The color matched the man's savage nature.

"You'd see the color your blood would run if the prime minister showed up here now. He paid his own price to possess those jewels. No doubt he still hunts the countryside for the thief."

A wicked, wide flash of yellowed teeth against his host's high cheekbones made Luther shudder. "Who does he search for?"

"No one of consequence. Some army sergeant named Phillip."

"A common name throughout the region." Janken clapped his hands, beaming. "You've earned the information you want." He raised his voice. "Innocent!"

The majordomo strode back into the room, a small stack of papers in hand. He set them in front of Luther and turned to leave.

"Thank you, Innocent." His host took a large bite of eggs.

"That's his name? An odd word to describe a hulking beast." *Unbelievable*.

"He bears the name of a Catholic saint, and my majordomo's mother held fierce religious beliefs, even if the spot between her thighs proved otherwise. All the information I received is there."

9

Luther riffled through the stack. Maps, soldier counts, sketches of layouts, and a short, sweet timeline. The last page brought the most attention. "They are carving out a tunnel to Britain?"

"Yes, and boasting it will be merely a trade route, but you're familiar with what comes next, *non*?" Janken swallowed another forkful of food.

The lack of conversation let the wheels rattle in Luther's head. Britain's leaders appeared to be turning stupid and willing to sacrifice common sense to prove to the world Germany wasn't an enemy. Only, they'd bet on the wrong horse. The kaiser's insatiable thirst for power, proven by his Nuremberg laws from a few years prior, stripped many across his dictatorship of their property and right to vote. Now this—the madness—had to stop.

"You neglected to mention your source."

"*Non, mon* Captain. Better to tell you after discovering the extent of this plot. It overshadows your *petite la femme* situation. There are worse things than potential assassinations." Janken nibbled a bite of bacon, took a sip of au lait, and still danced around the topic.

"Just tell me," Luther growled. He always attempted to keep his patience, since The Cursed did their best to beat it out of him. Once the group had prided itself on impatient, emotional-driven decisions. Since taking over, he'd been working his ass off to be better than his poor training, but, every once in a while, bad habits slipped back into place.

Janken shook his head. "Tsk. You're lucky I like you and your sister. Before I give you the information, I ask for a promise."

"What?"

"Will you honor it?" The albino drove hard bargains, but he'd never get a word out of the bastard without agreeing to his demands. The bastard had the upper hand.

"I honor nothing unless I want to. This is the way I do business, the way The Cursed does business. The rules have not changed."

The albino spat on the ground. "Screw The Cursed. We are not talking about business. This is personal. A request from *la mere* to one who owes her a debt."

Gooseflesh ran up his neck at the invocation of Janken's mother. He'd crossed her path once, and once proved to be one time too many. If the promise involved— "Name it."

The albino grinned, pleased. "Get Eva out of the camp and bring her home."

*Hell.* "Is she a prisoner?"

"Worse, she's been named a consort to the British engineer heading up the construction of the tunnel."

*Shit.* Ian had told him Eva got captured when the bounty hunter and Luther's sister escaped the British Embassy approximately six months ago, but he'd expected her to weasel her way out of it. Like she always did. The woman proved resilient in the face of anyone willing to attempt to stomp on her parade, including him. She'd also promised to sell him out if he didn't come for her, and now she'd turned consort. "I'll get her out. I can't promise I'll bring her home."

"We would be grateful if you did." An underlying threat lay within the low tones of his host's voice. Still scratchy, thanks to a love of cigarettes. In fact, Janken lit one now and took a drag. "*La mere* might host a dinner in your honor."

"Save your promises of my death. I won't transport anyone across the ocean against her will. I will rescue her, as repayment for my taking her from here in the first place." Luther picked up his cigar stub and shoved it into his mouth. "And I will offer to bring her here if she wants."

Then he rolled up the papers and stuffed them into a large pocket of his coat. The bulky material was lined with multiple pockets to give him a more significant appearance and keep those items dear to him near.

"Fine. I'll pass your message along. I take it you must leave now?" Janken took a long drag and flicked the ash into Luther's coffee cup. "No pleasure, then?"

"Plans to unravel this plot won't happen in this room. I'll need my crew at my disposal. Pleasure comes once I defeat my enemy."

"You mean Sauer?"

Luther laughed. "Damn straight. The fool will get what he deserves, and preferably it will involve two tons of bedrock at the entrance to this tunnel."

# Chapter Two

*Coquelles, France*

*"He was my north, my south, my east and west, My working week and my Sunday rest, My noon, my midnight, my talk, my song" – Funeral Blues, W H Auden*

And then he was gone. Standing on French soil again, watching the sun rise from her balcony perch, reminded her of a day etched into her mind permanently. The day Luther Corvino ditched her, in a town not far from here, citing idiotic reasoning about weakness and duty, and spouting false platitudes of coming back for her at some point when everything "died down." The same day she'd sworn off believing in men, trusting them.

But the saying went...*fool me twice, shame on me. Indeed.*

Eva had contacted him a little more than a year ago for help. Except, he'd done the opposite of providing help, which landed her in another cage, albeit gilded, working for the people responsible for the loss of her club and livelihood. Proving once more how the world enjoyed screwing over anyone searching for a break or with a moral compass.

She sipped her coffee, weak and watered. This was the best English prosperity could buy. Funny, since the Germans smuggled in the quality beans. At least she enjoyed tobacco. She took a long drag and flicked the ash over the side of the balcony wall. Taking pleasure where she could seemed the best route, along with biding her time until *they* determined her assignment complete.

Speaking of assignments, the door behind her creaked open. "Up with the sun, beautiful?"

"I'm an early riser, George."

"Most canaries are," he replied, pressing his body against the back of her chair and leaning down to kiss the top of her head. "Have trouble sleeping?"

She shook her head. "No, I just like to hear the birds sing, though I am serenaded by more seagulls and winds off the coast than anything. What are your plans today?"

Her British engineer, with his mop of ginger hair, took up position in the patio chair opposite her, grunting. "These damn things sit a bit low."

"Your plans?"

"Right, yes. There's a new shipment of workers coming in, from the south of France. Perfect really. We'll need more men to operate the new drills arriving later in the week."

Another drag finished off her cigarette. "Still on target?"

"Appears so. If there are no train delays, we'll be fine." He wrinkled his nose. "Smoking's a filthy habit, darling." He shielded his vision from the rising sun. George spent most of his time indoors or inspecting the inside of his growing tunnel. His lack of tolerance for being outside, in general, baffled her. "We may have to do some blasting."

"This filthy habit keeps me sane." Toying with a fresh cigarette, she tried to focus on the pleasure it would bring. She hated it when they blasted. Everything rattled, and she'd lost her favorite coffee cup to dynamite sticks blowing holes through rock. "How much blasting?" She didn't care how petulant the question sounded because being supportive on this topic remained beyond her.

George leaned over and patted her arm, his best effort at reassurance. The man acted less than amorous thus far. She could keep him satisfied with a little mouth action or a quickie in the majority of circumstances. No romantic efforts required. He abhorred them and enjoyed this quaint arrangement. They lived like an old married couple who stayed together for convenience, not love. "We're already over two football fields along in the tunnel. If we blast the edges of the wall to widen things out, it will make it easier for the drills. I can't guarantee no rumblies."

*Rumblies*. Another reminder of how George treated her as if she possessed a body and mind composed of glass or fine china.

He stood then leaned down to buss her cheek. "I can promise they won't be as loud or as harsh as the last few times."

"That will do, for now."

"For now, indeed. Another month and we'll be at the coast. Then you won't feel a thing."

"Are you going to put a miniature train system in?"

Opening the door to their room, he turned and grinned. "It will be much larger, dear."

"Then I'll feel everything."

George sighed. "You're witnessing history, Eva. My brother works on the opposite coast, doing the same thing I am. We'll meet in the middle in about nine months."

*Funny.* He'd said much the same three months prior. At this rate, the project would be more of a year's undertaking. George always provided plenty of excuses, too—not enough workers, a broken drill, poor weather, and unexpected dense bedrock.

"I've never been to England."

"You will be there soon enough. I'm off to breakfast." He disappeared then, all white shirt, suspenders, and khaki-colored pants paired with brown leather boots, headed off to the officer's tent. He mentioned her lack of cooking skills every so often. She'd been upfront about her weakness, and he'd taken it as one of those modest female moments. Until she'd burnt the first toast and cheese he'd asked her to make. George brought in hired help from Calais to prepare their meals, but for some reason liked to dine with the soldiers in the morning. His way of getting "chummy" with the soldiers.

She watched him get in his Jeep with one of their guards and drive away. *Time to get to work.*

Every morning, she did the same thing, like clockwork. First, the small domestic scene, followed by her report to the field marshal. Sauer believed all information to be important, even things she considered trivial. So, she wrote daily reports and sent them out in the hopes one of them would gain her release, regain her club. Then she dressed, did her hair and makeup, and went downstairs to deliver her report and get rid of the guard for a little while.

"Morning, Karl."

"Frau Eva." The handsome twenty-some man, in his military greens and cap, always stood ramrod straight at his post near the front door. He followed her outside, escorted her to the camp if she requested it, though she preferred to be away from the *workers*. Prisoners was a more accurate term, but such a word didn't sit well with the government's public relations department. She offered this morning's report to him. "Take this to the post for dispatch to Field Marshal Sauer."

"*Ja.*" He took the letter and marched out the door. She had exactly twenty minutes, another piece of her daily routine.

Twenty minutes granted her five to warm up and another fifteen to belt out five Delta blues tunes. The sad, soulful songs she had sung in the club in New Orleans. Songs her mama had taught her years ago. Her fingers hit the keys on the piano, more luck for her the house came with the instrument. Between the pedals, the ivory beneath her hands, and her voice, the memories flowed free. Ones she swore she wouldn't forget, about betrayal, heartache, and making deals with devils.

***

"You look a fright, boss." Roscoe's eyes drooped, and his normally happy face hung in a deep frown.

Luther outstretched his hand. "Give me a mirror. Did they get the color wrong?"

His first mate passed him the porthole-sized mirror. "No, but you don't look right. I mean, your beard's gone, and the hair—"

"It's exactly the way a German lieutenant is supposed to appear. I'm one of them, now. Where's the rest?"

"Here." Roscoe pointed at a glass bottle with a white liquid inside.

"I'll need to take it with me just in case my hair grows faster than planned." They'd traveled nonstop for two weeks, New Orleans to Iceland, and, now, nearly to the west coast of France. "Your job is to get south to my sister. She'll have the goods we need. Make sure to give her the note I drafted."

"Aye, Captain. I remember the instructions. We've gone over them ten times."

"You can never review things too many times." A philosophy that had paid off over the years. "In fact, let's run over the plan again. We make port at La Rochelle in approximately twenty minutes. Then Hans, Arik, and Dietrich will join me in our sudden German conscription on the train bound with new prisoners for Coquelles. Then you—"

"I will then direct the *Maledetto* to Corsica and your sister's ship *Liberte*. Where I'm to deliver your letter to her and then return with the goods. Will she refuse to help?"

Sorella still owed him for killing his contact with intimate knowledge of the tunnel plans. "No, she's aware of what will happen for denying help."

A horn sounded on the top deck, signaling their docking in the harbor. Then a knock on his cabin door. "Sir, a Django Reinhold requests permission to board."

"Granted. Show him in here when he's aboard." Luther stood and pulled off his black shirt, replacing it with a white tee and a forest-green button-down embroidered with a lieutenant's rank insignia. "We haven't gone over what will happen when you return."

"No, Captain." Roscoe poured three glasses of whiskey, no doubt in anticipation of their guest. Always a reliable man, his first mate proved indispensable when it came to dealing with guests or getting rid of them. In fact, he could stand in for Luther as a body double and had been growing his beard out in anticipation of the need. The exception was Roscoe's light-brown hair, in contrast to Luther's midnight-black shade, courtesy of his Italian ancestry. "We can discuss it now, if you'd prefer."

"Wait until our guest arrives." He absently reached for the beard he no longer sported and, instead, stroked a smooth chin. "Hell, and hand me a cigar."

Roscoe reached into his cigar box and pulled out a thick Cuban, clipped the end, and handed it to him along with a matchbook. Striking two matches always lit the cigar faster, and so Luther performed the action, puffing on the end until a steady stream of smoke drifted upward, and the sweet, intoxicating scent of burning tobacco filled the air. Horrible habits did produce some of the best relaxation tools, and, after a few drags on the half-inch thick tobacco leaf, a euphoric calm breached his troubled mind.

His first mate straightened the chairs to put his captain at the center of the conversation and their guest's back to the door. A wise move, and one to keep them in the dominant position. Around five minutes later, as Luther relaxed in his leather chair, uniform shirt unbuttoned, completely at ease, the door rattled then opened, and in strolled Django Reinhardt.

The man remained as hideous as the first time they'd met, with severe scarring on the left side of his face. He sported wavy, thick black hair slicked with pomade, along with a bushy mustache. The coins sewn into a fringe belt at his waist and the tops of his boots jingled as he crossed the room.

"Welcome, my gypsy friend. Have a seat. Care for a drink?"

Django's grin, as he sat down in a chair opposite Luther, did something atrocious to his scars. The man scared little children, no doubt. "Whiskey, if you have it. You changed up your image."

"Roscoe." He snapped his fingers, and his man jumped to attention. Gathering two glasses of whiskey, he distributed them. They always did things like this, playing up to the idea of the first mate being a servant. Hiding details had become essential in this new world of espionage and government overthrow.

His guest took a sip from the glass and let out a satisfied sigh. "Good stuff, but you always have the best. You sent me a letter wanting my help?"

"You still hate Germans?"

"The scars are still on my face."

Luther laughed. "Yes, they are. I've got a shipment of product coming in three weeks' time, if not sooner. I need someone to take hold of the cargo and bring everything to the encampment at Coquelles."

"You want to bring illegal contraband to the Germans building some damn tunnel, and you expect me to do it."

"It's the logical choice. You're already headed up there to entertain them and bring cigars and booze they won't get from supply trains. Besides, we're not going to leave the tunnel standing."

"What do you mean?" Django downed the rest of his drink and handed the glass to Roscoe for a refill. "The tunnel will be built whether we want it or not, and, afterward, we can expect a British bloodbath."

"Workers and equipment are needed, and I may not be able to stop it entirely, but I can cause a big fucking delay. There will be some experimental explosives and poison transported with these packages, which is why I need you. I can't have

Germans checking through everything. Your group can smuggle this stuff in, and friendship along with coin will ease the passage.

Django tapped his foot, revealing his nerves. Luther could relate, but winning the fight against the kaiser and getting a shot at killing the bastard who'd set his life on a bloodstained path to hell required great risks. "What's your issue with this plan?"

"You're asking me to endanger my entire family."

"I'll reward you handsomely." Coin, favors—he'd offer Django anything. "Just tell me what you want."

"I'm not sure yet, but it will be big when I figure it out." The man threw back his third whiskey. "For starters, you can give me one of those fancy cigars."

Roscoe cut a cigar, lit it, and handed it to Scarface.

Then Luther asked, "So you're in?"

"I'm in, which I'll probably regret, but you've pulled off some rather insane spectacles recently. I heard rumors the Germans are experimenting with silent, non-trackable airships. Care to confirm?"

*Damn*! No one could be trusted with classified information. People talked, from the engineers to the swabbies, and they always wanted to tell stories, especially after a few pints. "Rumors are rumors, and I can count on both hands how many times I meet crews sharing ridiculous stories in the hopes of presenting a tough presence."

Django grinned. "Sure, stay silent. So, where do I meet the shipment?"

"Here. The first mate will direct my ship to leave and pick everything up. Meanwhile, I and three others will infiltrate the camp, work on determining best areas to attack, and finalize a plan."

"Sneaky stuff. Getting around them won't be easy. There are lots of soldiers. Now, I see why you changed your face and hair. Smart move."

"Yes, I needed to look like them as much as possible." He hated it. Blond hair had never been his thing, or disguises, but, if needed, he'd do it. Originally, he'd planned to send in only the other three, but no one would be able to get through to Eva except him. "Speaking of the camp and the soldiers, I'm searching for someone."

"Man or woman?"

"Woman. Seen anyone interesting up there?"

Django shook his head and took another long drag from the cigar. Swirling cigar smoke hazed the air. "On the grounds near the tunnel and in the camp itself, there are only prisoner barracks, soldiers' barracks, the cook tent and mess, supply buildings, and a communications post. No women in any of those, but I haven't been to the engineer's house."

"Where's that?"

"Up on the hill. If anyone has a woman, it'd be the British upstart. Cordial as can be when it pleases him, but he's more interested in being the man who built the tunnel than worrying about the disaster it will bring."

Django's information matched what Janken had said. A beautiful canary imprisoned in some fancy cage. If Eva still resembled the woman who'd entranced him on the stage in New Orleans, she hated it. Such a bright star. She'd enjoyed performing, singing, and gaining the attention of others through her music. To play mistress to a man, especially one more interested in building tunnels than in her, would drive her nuts. She deserved every inch of the punishment if she'd sold any of his secrets, and he'd do his damnedest to find out what confessions she'd made and to whom.

"Thanks for the tidbit."

Another horn sounded from the top deck.

"My gypsy friend, I sense the time for talking is over. Our German inspectors will want to check my ship, and I'll need to be in complete disguise by then. I'll see you in a few weeks."

"*Oui*. Be safe, *mon ami*." Django turned to leave, and, for a moment, Luther believed in the sincerity of his words, unlike Janken's sharing of the the sentiment.

"I'll do my best," he replied, tossing his captain's hat to Roscoe. After which he grabbed the end of his shirt, tucking the corners into his trousers. In no time, he transformed himself into a German soldier ready for battle. The scowl fit the ensemble, but the cigar had to go.

He took the stub, long out of flame and suffocated by the lack of oxygen, and dropped it into an ashtray. "How do I look?"

Roscoe approached and gave him a pat on the shoulder. "Like a wolf in ass's clothing."

Luther grinned. "Let's go."

***

The last few notes of her bluesy song echoed off the walls in the parlor. Eva picked up her cocktail from the piano top, let her foot off the muffler pedal, and downed the vodka martini fast. A kitchen boy immediately came from the corner to retrieve her glass and make her another one.

Full glass in hand, she decided to abandon the cleaning servants, soldiers, and smells of the roast dinner for a solitary moment in her room. Said moment evolved into several minutes of smoking a cigarillo on the terrace. She stood there puffing and exhaling rings of smoke, watching the sun dip lower, now blazing a path of heat on her left arm instead of the right one. She started to hum the sounds of "La Vie En Rose"longing for her club, the marquee lights, and the crowds they'd start to draw as the evening set in. Ownership of her entire setup ripped away from her due to a stupid law, along with her ability to save the folks who worked for her.

She'd been promised a chance to save them for a deal with the devil. *Damn.* Another drag and she mused on her friends. Had Carmela birthed her baby yet? Had Benito or Henri found additional work, or given up on her and everyone else for a chance at regular rations by joining the German army?

A train whistle blew in the distance, and the monstrous, black engine rolled into the camp, much to her dissatisfaction. Multiple cars carried workers, supplies, and food, as George had promised, as well as his big drills. Her engineer would be a happy boy tonight. She shuddered at the depressing idea of another boring conversation about drilling and tunnel building.

Trains had become essential German transport over the years, especially for big shipments. Airships, thanks to Tesla, provided quicker transport. Though, according to George, rumors about Tesla's engine falling prey to innovations in hydrogen research ran rampant among those in high society. George revealed himself as a technology addict, always interested in discussing improvements and technological advances. An area she knew little about, which made his admiration of her suspect.

As the steam hissed, the brakes screeching to a halt, soldiers gathered near a pair of cars, electo wands at the ready. Hopefully on the stun setting. The doors slid open on their tracks, and prisoners fell, tripped, and collapsed onto the built-up dirt platform alongside the train. Many rubbed their eyes, further proof, beyond their ghostly pallor, they'd been denied even sunlight during transport.

Her spot on the hill granted her an unobstructed view, and she could imagine the smell, the pain as the soldiers zapped at them, poking and prodding like cattle. It brought back memories of wandering the streets of New Orleans with foul odors of excrement, tobacco, and alcohol souring the air. Of being baited and captured by a woman who put her on the selling block, though no one purchased her, and being rescued by a voodoo queen. These poor folks wouldn't be so lucky, and no way she'd risk her neck for them. People counted on her, ones of her personal acquaintance, not a car full of strangers.

A rap sounded on the door. "Watching the sunset, beautiful?"

She chuckled. Such a fool. Her engineer probably had never experienced a hungry, dirty moment in his life. At least not one he hadn't arranged. "Yes, a beautiful view, but interrupted by the awful train."

"A necessary evil," he said with no care or concern for the plight of the humanity at the bottom of the hill.

"Necessary, like the prisoners transported here to work. The ones who got locked up for being hungry, for losing homes, or daring to stand up to tyranny." She couldn't help the anger and outrage bubbling up inside. The glimmering moment where she compared herself to them—stuck and enslaved.

"Don't start the same old tantrum. These people lost their freedom for breaking laws established by

31

their government, but, here, they get a chance to earn it back through hard work."

Eva scoffed, "The lies you tell yourself are quite humorous." Refusing to give him any more attention, she kept her back turned and deliberately crushed the lit end of her cigarillo against the stucco, leaving a big, black streak that matched the one on her soul.

George approached and grasped her by the upper arms. Turning her slowly toward him, he leaned down, putting his face level with hers. Pure strength. The man possessed little of much else, but his body was honed. "I hate it when you're mad at me. But I can't do any more than give those people a purpose beyond rotting in a prison cell. Please don't be angry with me because two governments don't have a better solution."

She struggled at first but then relaxed in his hold. In a way, his words made sense. If he'd refused to work on the project out of moral reasoning, they would've found someone else, perhaps a man who'd have beaten her. "Sorry for getting worked up. It bothers me."

"I don't care for it, either, but sometimes we have to sacrifice our attitudes and preferences for the greater good." He pressed a kiss to her forehead. "Let's go down for dinner. There's a special dessert in store."

Those brief moments, when his hazel eyes softened and his need to please her reared its head, she wanted to tell him the truth. Wanted— "George, sweetheart?"

He let go of her and took a step back. "Yes? What's wrong?"

The words sat on there on the tip of her tongue, but survival instinct kept them locked in place. "You're too good to me."

"I hope so because I plan to do more once we complete this tunnel. You've bewitched me." They left the terrace, but she still didn't feel content. No, guilt ate at her, but she stuffed it down with roasted potatoes, turnips, and a healthy slice of beef. Eating real food, real portions, fell within the category of surviving, and she'd sacrifice a little more self-respect for the comfort her lies won her.

Luther huddled toward the back of the train, on top of the caboose. The train's cupola allowed him a bird's-eye view. He aimed the binoculars mounted to the top of the box toward the house on the hill. A beautiful chateau with at least a dozen rooms, but what caught his eye the most—the woman on the upper terrace staring at him with a haunted look in her eyes. For a moment, he believed she might have seen him, but then he realized her gaze followed the prisoners emerging from the cars at the front of the train. She appeared a bit thinner than he remembered, but her beauty had become more pronounced, and the green, serviceable dress she wore hid her gorgeous curves.

A ginger-haired man, dressed in khakis and a white shirt, stepped out. They started talking, no, arguing, if the frown on Eva's face could be believed. She turned away, smashing her cigarette against the railing and, when he grabbed her arm, Luther growled. *Damn.* No one would touch her in a rough fashion again, ever, and the bastard would be getting a taste of Luther's fist before he finished here. After Eva gave him what for.

Except…she didn't. No, she fell in line and, when the dandy let go and pressed a kiss to her forehead, Luther punched the wall, leaving a dent. Sure, he didn't want his secrets spilled, but his Eva never backed away from a fight, never gave in. Her feisty nature had drawn him, even back then.

"Sir." The whisper came from the back of the caboose.

Luther looked down the ladder. "Yes, Arik."

"They are calling for all soldiers on board to assemble on the platform."

"I'll be down in a second." One quick peek through the telescope lens, and he discovered the pair had magically disappeared. Priority became making contact with her, one way or another, after he'd familiarized himself with the camp and confirmed intelligence. "And, if she's been beaten, I'll kill the bastard."

# Chapter Three

The next morning, after Luther rolled himself out of the hard, low-to-ground cot and shaved away his scruff, he found his team. The four of them wandered into the mess tent, the fog still rolling in from the coast outside and the sun barely inching over the horizon.

Armies were predictable—breakfast before dawn, everyone required to eat with those switching off night duty. They grabbed their tin plates with oat mush, a sausage link, and a wedge of orange. Weak coffee in tin cups accompanied the standard fare, which would be repeated for lunch if the grumbling from other soldiers turned out to be accurate.

Instead of seating themselves among the soldiers, Luther and his men shuffled outside to enjoy their meal from a small hill across from the tent. Luther chose to stand versus sit, and he kept a keen eye on the tent flaps for any others who may be attracted to their little group.

"Where are you stationed?"

Arik spoke first. "They've put me on a post guarding supplies and handling any trains in or out."

Outside of Roscoe, he'd worked with this man the longest. The pale-blond had been kidnapped by The Cursed on an excursion into Sweden shortly before Luther joined the *Maledetto*.

"You, Dietrich?" He tried a swig of the coffee and nearly spit it out. The mix tasted weak and old like the grounds got reused over and over.

"Captain—"

"That's not my rank. Get it right, or you'll have an accident." This type of mission could afford no mistakes.

"Sorry, Lieutenant. I've got duty on the tunnel itself, supervising workers and equipment in and out." Still a soldier at heart, the mustached fool shoveled in the food without hesitation.

"Starting to feel at home, Diet?"

"Never. Home is where your family lives, and mine is dead." It was the exact reason the defected German had come to The Cursed—for revenge, much like the majority of newer crew members. They sought to play a role in the empire's destruction.

Arik had already finished his meal and gawked at Luther's as if he'd never eaten a crumb. "You plan on eating your food, sir?"

"No, eat away." Luther handed the poor excuse for breakfast over and turned his attention to his last man. "Hans, give me the good news."

The man sported a bit of red in his hair but still held enough blond to pass for a member of the Motherland of Europe. For this mission, he'd donned fake glasses to make himself seem less capable of tasks involving good eyesight. "Our plan worked. They've put me on prisoner guard duty. I start the night shift in a few days, which works out well."

He'd learned a few things, too. "It appears my intelligence is correct and we have a female agent working as a spy and stationed as a consort to the chief engineer. We need to get someone, preferably me, on duty in the house."

Luther fell silent as a group of ten men emerged from the tent, laughing and lighting cigarettes. The image reminded him of his need for a little something extra, and he pulled out a cigar. He'd only brought a few with him, but chewing on the end of one sufficed for now. "Hans, you start night shift this evening?"

"*Ja.*" They'd practiced plenty of German in preparation for the trip. It made sense they'd use it.

"Then get on up to the house and arrange an accident. I need someone gone."

38

Hans nodded and handed his half-full plate off to Dietrich, who like Arik, gobbled the food. "It will be done."

As Hans tramped off to follow orders, Luther spoke to the remaining men. "How can you eat the crap they serve here?"

"It's sustenance," Dietrich replied, words slightly muffled by the mush in his mouth. Once he'd swallowed, he continued, "Soldiers learn fast that food can be scarce in times of war. So you eat when you can and whatever you can. As long as we're not cooking rats, I'm good."

Being in black market mercenary work spoiled him. He ate like a king most of the time, and, before his ransom, he'd lived with a privileged family and wanted for nothing, except love. "I'll keep that in mind." And he'd pray lunch proved to be anything besides more of the same.

***

Another report finished, Eva glided down the stairs, ready to eat her breakfast of eggs and sausage. She'd grown tired of mush, and George now demanded eggs and other breakfast options for her. If anyone despised her for being spoiled, they never said.

"This is for the post, Karl."

He took her letter and tucked it into a coat pocket. Same thing, every day.

"Karl?"

"Yes, Frau Sonne?" The young man reached for the door handle to leave.

"When did you join the military?" Her thoughts continued to be maudlin. This one seemed so nice, so innocent.

"I became a soldier to uphold the legacy of the German people. The military offers such a chance. I enlisted at age ten."

She almost gasped but held firm. They conscripted at ten years old. "Did you leave home then?"

"I got sent to school. Parents cannot afford to feed all their young. I had three sisters with hungry mouths. I did my duty. More food came with my service. I go to send the message now, Frau Sonne." He marched out, shutting the door gently behind him.

Such a horrible life, reared to feel honor bound to or to believe in duty. Where sons sacrificed their futures to feed their starving families. No one over in America heard these things, but a person learned quickly on European soil, especially when meals became crumbs. How the Germans continued to be hailed as bringing order to chaos baffled her.

Sitting down at the piano, she started in on a Gershwin tune, hoping to chase her blues away. Instead, the room shook briefly, and a breakfast plate rattled on the small table to her left. A glass fell to the floor due to the force of a blast far too close.

She launched off the bench, pulling her robe tight around her as she ran out the front door. Not even sixty meters away, the car Karl used to drive into the camp sat burning. Flames licked the air like whips seeking purchase from an invisible source, and she could make out the shape of Karl's body being consumed by the fire. She'd expected screams, cries for help, some reaction, but the soldier remained still.

She watched the fire burn, the tires melt into liquid, and the steel cage sink toward the ground. Only then did the shouts of men and the rumble of another car engine cut through her concentrated focus.

A man in a cap, with a gigantic frame blocking out the sun, asked about her health, her state of being. She nodded absently at him, then the soldier turned away and shouted orders. Those included searching the house. The fog cleared immediately. No one needed to touch her things, especially her clothes or her writing materials. *Damn it.*

"There's no need to search anything."

"Frau Sonne, someone attacked the Jeep and this man. He may be hiding in the house. Or possibly you've got some contraband they want." The soldier shuffled off, leaving her in the drive. The stupid fools didn't care about anything except their own crazy theories. They probably got off on the idea of going through her clothing since they were deprived of female companionship.

Another volunteered to escort her inside. She didn't like him either. She wanted Karl back. Sweet and somewhat innocent, he'd never raised his voice or done anything untoward. This one studied her like he wanted to eat her, all leering hazel eyes and smarmy grin.

Then the broad-chested soldier returned. "Enough! Get down the hill and round up some men to search the fields beyond the house. We need to make sure someone wasn't trying to get to the engineer."

She turned her gaze on the firm, tall male specimen beside her. No one called George "the engineer." They addressed him as Herr Buckner. Every time. Her protector ordered the men to check the kitchens, the gardens, and everywhere else imaginable. He was a typical blond, blue-eyed German, but the scar trailing down his left cheek struck a chord. She recognized this man from somewhere but couldn't say where.

"Let me help you inside."

"I think I can get there on my own, thank you," she replied taking a few steps back to get a better vantage point.

He stepped in close. "My little canary, it's best we get you indoors."

She stiffened as memories flooded her. Those black eyes, the moment they met. Her on the stage belting out something about love being for fools. He'd stood there, a predatory gaze focused and intent. Instinct had her taking brisk steps to get as far away from the man who'd made her act an idiot all those years ago. Why the hell— How the hell did he get here?

Escape failed when her slipper snagged on a rock, and he grabbed her arm and held her upright. He'd always been able to move her around like a ragdoll, but, in this instance, he didn't let go. Instead, he guided her into the house, across the foyer, and leaving her by the piano bench.

"Sit," he commanded as he closed the doors, shutting them into to the room alone. "We'll need some privacy."

His firm, assured steps brought him back to her side. Where had he come from? How had he found her? She'd once thought of him as her hero, her personal one. When he hauled her up into his arms, she closed her eyes, the savage kiss he placed on her lips stirring up an arousal she hadn't experienced since he'd stranded her on this godforsaken continent.

She melted into his familiar embrace. Knocking his cap from his head, she twined her fingers in his hair, their tongues dancing. He groaned. Then passion fell away to reality, to hard truths. Eva bit his lip, and he dropped her. Luckily, she possessed enough sense to land on her feet.

"You're not happy to see me?"

Growling, she hauled off and slapped him. "Go to hell."

"I think I'm already there."

He'd wanted to kiss her as soon as he'd spied her from the train and, once he got her alone, decided to take advantage of the situation like any decent mercenary would. She'd reacted as expected, falling against him. Too bad her initial emotions lasted for such a short time. His cheek stung, but, if he got his way, she'd earn the punishment back soon enough.

"Hit me again and then it will be my turn."

Her hand flew toward his face again, but this time he caught it. "You still believe it's all right to hit women."

He chuckled and released her hand. "If a woman asks for them, I believe spankings are well deserved."

Eva groaned and moved toward the window. A knock on the foyer door interrupted them, and he cursed under his breath.

"Come."

The door opened without a sound, perfectly oiled, unlike his own ship's doors. "Sir, we searched the house and found no signs of an intruder or illegal trespasser. Things appear safe here."

"Good." Luther approached the soldier, summoning his full height and deepest commanding voice. "I'll stay here until someone else more qualified can be appointed."

"More qualified?"

"This woman's life may be in jeopardy. Not just any soldier should stand guard. She'll need someone highly trained." And a hell of a lot more educated than the poor, young idiot Hans had dispatched without a fight. He'd watched his man launch himself into the truck, stab the soldier, stop the vehicle, and rig an explosion in under two minutes. Whoever chose the guard for Eva didn't give a shit if she ended up dead or not.

"Excuse me, sir?" He closed the short distance between him and the soldier. "She's never been assigned a trained specialist to guard her. They don't deem her important enough."

"She's important to the engineer?" His question came out a whisper to match the low-level tones of the idiot beside him.

"Herr Buckner?"

"Is there any other engineer here?" he yelled.

"No, sir." The soldier jumped back, and Eva giggled behind him.

"Then I'm speaking of the one and only. She's important to him and therefore requires protection. As I'm the highest ranking officer here, and the most qualified, I'll fill the role until further direction is provided. Understand?"

The boy rocked his wobbly legs straight and delivered a piss poor salute. Luther then gave additional orders. "Get everyone back to their regular duties, except for a two-man team to put the car fire out and get medical to dispose of the body."

"Yes, sir. Heil, Kaiser." He marched off, shutting the door behind him.

Luther turned, grabbing his cigar from his pocket then sticking it into his mouth to chew on. Better to occupy his lips with something other than kissing this spitfire again. No, he needed information. "So, you got caught in the embassy?"

She grabbed the sides of her robe, and tucked them over one another, hiding her yellow silk nightgown, then tied the sash. "Thanks to your sister."

"You could've turned her away."

"I've only met two people capable of being so cruel. Janken and you."

Test number one, and she'd passed it. "How did they get you?"

She turned toward the front window with its view of the small copse of trees on the other side of the drive. "They would've gotten me no matter what, but I appeared more valuable than a typical stage performer thanks to your sister shooting me in the arm. She gave the impression I was a liability to her, and, therefore, the Germans kept me for interrogation."

"And what did you tell them?"

Glancing over her shoulder, she flashed a saucy grin. "Wouldn't you like to know?"

The woman infuriated him. *Damn her*. "You'll tell me, or I'll make sure you won't talk anymore."

She looked around the room.

"There's nothing close enough to grab before my knife flies." Luther grabbed the hilt of his blade. "What you told them, quickly."

She sighed. "I revealed your Iceland location and confirmed your sister's existence aboard her ship. My information passed to a Colonel Altenbach, but...since you're here, he must be dead."

"Dear sister dispatched him for me. Anything else?" She'd been the reason for the stealth attack. Thankfully, his sister's decision to spare lives and spread stories worked in their favor. German forces believed Altenbach's test craft had perished in a fire on Luther's small island, taking all the dissidents with them, with the exception of those on the *Maledetto*.

"Nothing else. What more could I say? We never swapped secrets. No, I got sent here to spy on the British engineer heading up the tunnel. My only other option was to join the prisoners."

"Why you?" He ground his teeth against his cigar.

"The man took a fancy to me at one of the British embassy balls and wasted plenty of breath letting everyone know. He believes me to be kind, considerate, and in need of a calm, relaxed environment."

The bounder was dead wrong. Eva had never wanted such things. Had she changed? "You wanted this cage?"

"It's nice eating well every night and not worrying about someone busting down my door or following me home in the hopes of getting something special."

The urge to ask when the hell all this crap had taken place took fierce hold of him. He tamped it down just as the roar of the Jeep engine cut off outside. If he stayed in the room when the idiot came in, he'd hit the bastard. Better to leave and continue the conversation tomorrow. "Great sob story. We'll talk more tomorrow."

"What?" She frowned, eyes blaring hatred. "You're an ass."

"So I've been told. Nothing new. You're beautiful." He peeked out the window to see the ginger-haired fool hop out of the Jeep and stroll slowly toward the door. *Real concerned, this one.* "See you tomorrow. Hopefully, wearing more clothes."

"Sure you don't want to introduce yourself to my lover, the man keeping me warm at night?"

"Rather be dunked in a mine swamp off the coast. Dream of me." He opened the doors leading into the dining room. "See you in the morning."

"Not if you're arrested first."

The front door opened, and a deep British voice called out, "Eva?"

Luther paused. "You haven't even listened to my proposal."

"Why should I?" She played with a strand of her hair. The foyer doorknob rattled.

"It will get you the hell away from here and more."

# Chapter Four

Eva stared at her reflection in the mirror, thankful her mocha skin helped hide her tired eyes. She'd tossed and turned, finally giving up on sleep and spending her night huddled on a terrace chair with a blanket, a glass of sherry, and her cigarillos. She'd contemplated her situation, replaying her entire conversation with Luther, formulating her questions until the birds began to chirp. A robin landed above her on the eaves, singing its morning calls, and she nearly joined in but decided to rise instead.

Time better spent readying for battle, exactly what any conversation with her ex-lover turned into—another skirmish in a long heartbreaking war. Too bad she'd been unable to figure out how to distance herself from her feelings completely. Today meant a new day to try again, another chance to cut her heart out and hide it in a box.

After a bath in hot, steaming water, she donned a cream flower-patterned silk sheath dress that defined her curves. She put her hair up in a ponytail before using the iron to create perfect long curls, floating down to skim her neck. She applied the final touches, kohl around her eyes, a bit of blush on her cheeks, and a spritz of her favorite perfume. The final touch, her magnetic necklace, a gift and a weapon from the original owner of her nightclub, Madame Le Roux, but she'd never used it, never reflected about it more than as a memento of her home.

"You're done up fancy today," George said from behind her. He wore his usual outfit, all crisp white, khaki, and clean. His hair was combed to the left and still damp. "What's the occasion?"

"No reason. A girl needs to get gussied up every once in a while."

"You're a gorgeous dish, and everyone sees it, including me. Remember, you don't need anything flamboyant to impress me. I like you plain Jane or dressed up. Either works." He leaned in to kiss her cheek. The contact reminded her of Luther's forceful kiss from the day before. She wanted the same from George. Passion. He'd professed his desire for her to dozens of people yet never showed any passionate response.

"George?" She turned on her bench to face him as he moved away.

"Yes?"

"Kiss me before you leave."

"I did."

She stood and approached him. Looping her arms around his neck, she whispered, "No, kiss me." Pressing her lips to his, she traced his with her tongue. He finally wrapped his arms around her waist and opened to her, but his response still lacked fire.

Pulling back, he smiled. "Definitely a good way to send a man off to work. I'll see you soon."

Once removed from their embrace, he straightened his shirt and left. *Damn.* She deserved his disregard for trying to trade one person for another. George took care of her, which should've been enough. Too bad her body and brain wanted more.

Once he drove off in the Jeep, Eva went downstairs. She paused outside the small parlor without the piano and asked the maid to serve her breakfast in that room. Before too long, a maid came in with her meal. As the maid poured her coffee, Luther stalked in, face in a permanent frown and his hat crooked on his head. She'd never get over those blond locks. In fact, she hated them.

"Morning, Lieutenant. Care for some coffee?"

He groaned. "No, I've already had my cup of watered-down grounds."

No sense in volunteering her cup contained chicory coffee from New Orleans, smuggled in at George's request. He could suffer a bit. "Suit yourself." She poured from the pot, and then he leaned a bit, sniffing at the air like a hound dog.

"I might be thirsty after all."

"Too bad. There's only one cup, and soldiers aren't allowed to fraternize with me."

Luther grinned. "I'll sip off yours."

"I'll throw this pot at your head first."

He laughed before sitting down in the chair across from hers. A small table separated them, and a part of her wanted to demand he move, but doing so would give her feelings away. Infuriating.

She chose to ignore him, sipping on her coffee before starting in on her English muffin and jam.

"You honestly eat those British rocks?"

"When in Rome." The muffin crunched between her teeth, and the sweet taste of blueberry jam touched her tongue. Delicious, heavenly muffins, especially when toasted just right. As she chewed, eyes closed, gooseflesh broke out on her arms. He watched her, and the fact he did unnerved her. "Quit it. Stare at something besides me."

"Why? You've gotten all dressed up, which means you want the attention."

"I did this for me, and I would've yesterday if my morning hadn't been interrupted." She took another bite and quickly washed it down with her sweet coffee. "You mentioned a proposal. Out with it, before I decide you're not worth the trouble."

"You think you're safe in this house, with your engineer. Think I can't implicate you as soon as you deliver me to your lover. I may have already planted something damning in this house to make you guilty of spying on him."

"There lies the mistake with your plan. I'm already a spy for the Germans, and they will come to my rescue far faster than they will come to yours." Challenge her and be damned. No way in hell could he jeopardize her position in the household. All he could do was make her angry enough to have him disposed of.

"Fine. Proposal, then. After I get a taste of your coffee."

"You probably have some sort of disease."

"If I do, you've got it, too, since we kissed yesterday. Hand the cup over." He grinned at her and took off his hat. "I'll take a small swallow."

She couldn't help but return the same grin she'd spent so much time with. A grin charming enough to convince her to leave her life in New Orleans for a big adventure, one which had landed her here, in this crappy place. By the time he handed the cup back, her smile had turned sour. For her peace of mind, they need to wrap this up. "The proposal?"

"What is your role as a spy?"

More questions, never answers. "I write reports on tunnel progress and have them sent to General Field Marshal Sauer. He's the kaiser's right-hand man and has taken a personal interest in this project. He wants news on everything about supply trains, blasting, whatever George tells me."

"When do you send these reports?"

"Every day, until yesterday when you blew up Karl."

Another partial grin and he poured a stream of coffee into her cup. "I didn't blow up...Karl, you called him. Unfortunately, I can't take responsibility for the accident."

"Then one of your crew did it. Nonetheless, my last report went up in flames, and once a report doesn't show up, it will get Sauer worried. It may even bring him here." She didn't like the man. His beady black eyes, hooked nose, and thinning hair—along with his dismissive tone and rude behavior. He cared about nothing except dominating the entire world and convincing the kaiser to do it.

Luther added cream then sugar, and stirred everything in, as she liked it. "What about today's report? Do you have it ready?"

"I didn't write one. Why should I? You're not going to deliver it."

"Of course I am, after you add in some information about things not happening as they should." He handed the cup to her, and she took a drink. Perfect. He'd remembered how she liked her coffee. That shouldn't be a big deal. She shouldn't make it one.

"You seem to forget I want you gone."

"Help me get Sauer here, and I'll be gone, along with you."

She set the cup down and linked her hands together. "Why do you want him so bad?"

"Because I'm going to kill him."


In his experience, telling the truth was a trait one employed only when necessary. But he'd always found it hard to lie to Eva. More so when she tossed aside her sassy, combative nature for the quiet, demure side she liked to deploy on him periodically.

"You?" She chuckled, "He's been the right-hand of the kaiser since the middle of the World War. He helped convince Tesla to join the other side. He creeps me out and scares the hell out of me. How could you kill him?"

"By not pretending he's invincible for starters? The man's made of flesh and blood like you, like me. Why can't I kill him?"

A knock sounded at the door, and Eva shook her head, her face still stuck in the same condescending expression, like he'd lost his mind. "Come."

The door opened, and a servant walked in. "This just arrived for you, Frau Sonne. I'll take the dishes as well, if you're done." She handed over a large box into Eva's outstretched hands, took the breakfast tray, including the coffee, and left.

Luther hadn't bothered to rise from his seat, nor did he give a damn if the stupid woman reported his presence to the Brit. "Expecting something?"

"Nothing, actually." She tossed the lid to the side and pulled back the layers of tissue paper to reveal some brown-and-pink monstrosity with a belt. Buttons ran up the side. It was something his mother would've worn. Shapeless and not very flattering.

"You ordered a hideous dress?"

"No," she replied absently, pulling a card out of the box. "I received a gift from George. He drove to Calais a few days ago for supplies, and this dress caught his eye. He meant to be attentive and it fit me, with a few alterations."

He scoffed. "The fool has no genius fashion sense. Best he keeps to his building projects."

"At least he attempts to show caring and appreciation for me, unlike other men."

The woman always brought up the past. "I didn't hear you complaining when I pleasured you at night, and my wealth didn't put me a position to flatter with gifts. You want gifts? I'll fill this place with dead bodies and let you dance over them to freedom."

"Is this what you think I want?"

"Freedom, yes. Can you honestly tell me you're happy in this cage? Given ridiculous gifts when you want the ability to come and go as you please?" He paused and stood. As he stepped closer to her, the box fell onto the floor where it landed with a thump. "Do you still play the songs you love, or has the German oppression stopped those as well? Can you be you without hiding?"

She leaned back and pressed herself against the chair as if trying to escape him. "I'm safe and secure."

"Until they are done using you."

"Or until you are," she spat back. The gold flecks in her eyes flashed always in anger now versus the passion they'd once held. A fine line to tread.

He narrowed his own at her. "Why do you always fight me?"

"Why do you show up where you're not wanted?"

Pounding his palms against the armrests of her chair, he fought the urge to kiss her into submission. It worked in the past, and, honestly, it was either do something physical or threaten violence. *Damn, her.* Instead, he roared and backed away. "Have a report ready for tomorrow. I'll be back then."

He slammed doors behind him, getting outside, and relished the fresh air while lighting a new cigar. She always set him off, had conducted the research early on in their relationship on what drove him crazy. The buttons to push, the easy way to guide him from rational and calm to pissed and irate. Even when he'd promised to free her, to kill anyone who stopped their escape, she still chose to be obstinate and fight him.

What the hell did she hold back? He nearly turned around to go back and ask.

Instead, he stomped down the hill, toward the camp, puffing on his cigar, contemplating. The few citizens in his path cleared out of his way. Contemplating their interaction and the lack of moving forward on any plan, he needed to get through to her and get her to come around to his thinking. By now, Roscoe had to be close to finding Sorella. They'd been gone three days, and the *Maledetto* traveled fast, faster than most ships. Had to, to keep up with their reputation.

It wouldn't take more than a couple of weeks, including delays if storms popped up or extra German patrols occurred, etc., for everything to arrive. He needed the general here by then, aggravated and within Luther's grasp.

When he finally reached Hans' tent, he stormed inside, the anger still not completely gone. "Report."

Hans scrambled out of bed, stumbling over his own feet. "Sir, night shift boasts fewer soldiers. There's a gap in security at the witching hour. Maybe late night gambling, but I intend to find out."

The report trailed on, but his focus broke at the sound of someone with a British accent weaving in and out of the tents.

"Hold there. I'll be back in a moment." Luther left the tent and weaved in between the other ones until he lined up to a ginger-headed fool, two inches shorter than himself, reviewing equipment reports with two other lieutenants. "Excuse me, are you the British engineer?"

Ol' red hair turned and gave him a side glance. A bit dismissive, this one. "Yes, and I have a name. Most call me by it."

"Afraid I'm new here."

George, as she called him, stopped his conversation and turned to face him. "They call me Herr Buckner, and, as you can see, I'm busy. Something you need?"

"Are you at all concerned about Frau Sonne's well-being?"

Ginger pulled back, screwing his face up. "I don't see how that's any business of yours."

"Security is a little lax. She's watched over by a single guard during the day and one at night. Someone killed her previous guard."

"Most likely a petrol accident. These things can happen. Besides, what do you care about some *mulatto*?"

The last word had Luther clenching both fists and biting down so hard on his cigar, little embers sprinkled onto the ground. "Just checking your loyalties, Herr. Can't be too careful."

"She's amusement. I understand you're not afforded the luxury in your position, but I am. You'd be better off sending more protection for me. It's most likely me they're after."

"Would you like us to provide more guards?"

The Brit paused for a minute, stroked his red scruff-covered chin and then, with a nod, replied, "No. I think we're fine. Now, stick to your duties and let me tend to my own."

"*Ja*, Herr Buckner." Luther ground out the last words, and it choked him to do so. If he had a chance, the bastard would die from a knife wound to the chest.

\*\*\*

For dinner, Eva wore the new frock. The shapeless, brown, pink— *what had Luther called it?*— hideous dress made her look disfigured in a way, but

63

she didn't want to insult the man who gave it to her or the intent behind the gift.

She smiled on her way into the parlor. George stood near her piano, drink in hand, and fiddled with a few of the high note keys. He glanced up at her entrance and grinned. "You're radiant."

*Really?* Her attempt to exude happiness faltered. "Thank you again for the gift."

"Let's not ruin the moment with overrated flattery. The brown matches your skin and creates this artistic effect. Truly. Did you want a cocktail before dining?" He sounded so proud of himself, and inside her stirred a kernel of anger.

"No, I'm famished. Let's go in."

"We'll wait a minute so I can finish my drink. Martinis don't sit well with food." Normally, he didn't drink such a thing, preferring a glass of wine and post dinner port.

The cue for her to start talking. "Stressful day?"

He sat down on her bench, set his glass on the piano top, and reached for her. She went into his outstretched arms. "You always recognize when things have been tough or good. You read me well. Stressful isn't the right word, frustrating or worrisome sounds more accurate. One of the drills on the machine jammed, and it took the better part of the day to fix it. We only drilled half the quota. At this rate, we may need to run nights a couple of times this week."

"Will the workers be hurt?"

"No, we'll split them into two groups to keep them from being worn out and drag in some of the German soldiers to help if needed in the drilling and hauling. The work must be done." He paused, squeezing her a bit tighter against him. "Then, with everything yesterday, the blown up Jeep and the dead soldier, my concentration hasn't been as steadfast. The fool of a lieutenant confronting me didn't help either."

George let go of her then, gently urging her with his palms to move away. He threw back the rest of this drink and let out a sigh. She kept her best poker face and waited to hear more of this story. No doubt Luther had done something stupid, something to play to her advantage.

"Did you see this man?"

She raised her eyebrows and pursed her lips. "Who?"

"A lieutenant. Blond hair, black eyes. Surly?" He rose from the bench and moved to make another drink. Whatever Luther had done, it had upset him, put him on edge.

"I can't tell them apart, but a lieutenant did stop by today and inform me he'd been assigned as my new guard. He seemed a bit infatuated, even too careful. Didn't want to leave my side. He possessed a set of broad shoulders. I mean, a bigger top half." She shrugged hers to make light of the topic. "No big thing."

George leveled a serious frown at her. "Did he make any advances?"

"No, of course not. He's most likely a bit sweet on me. Flattering, really." She sat on the bench and pressed in a few keys, the start to a low, soft melody. One he'd commented on liking before. "I wouldn't worry too much."

He moved in closer, blocking out the light from the lamps positioned around the fireplace behind them. "I don't like it. In fact, maybe I should request he be moved to another post."

In the past, she'd always enjoyed close contact with George. She even enjoyed the warmth his body gave to her, but her ex-lover's arrival had poisoned the presence of the engineer. Even now, she forced herself to stay relaxed and not tense as he touched her back. Her reactions to him were in complete opposition with her mission to stay close.

She clucked and shook her head, continuing to stroke the ivory underneath her fingertips for musical notes to imitate calm and serenity. "You should be grateful someone cares as much about my safety as you do."

"But he accused me of the opposite. In reality, who would want to hurt you? Most likely the attack was a potential threat to my own person." The words hurt, as if somehow his existence superseded the importance of hers.

That kernel of anger ignited and began to expand. She hit the wrong note. "Of course. You are the key to Germany's success with this project."

He patted her on the shoulder. "Right you are. The fool had the gall to think you were somehow the one threatened, over the fact it could've been me driving the Jeep. The bomb likely got planted in the evening. Lucky for me, I drive the other one, but how humiliating for the assassin. They can't even get their target right."

*Oh!* She fumed, the anger now burst, spreading through her veins like the very fire from the exploded Jeep. Up until now, she'd believed George to be a bit narcissistic, but never this self-absorbed. Care for her well-being appeared more myth than reality. "I'm not feeling well, dear. I think I might skip dinner this evening."

"It might make you feel better. We're having offal and mushy peas with mint sauce."

The idea of trying another one of his British delicacies made her stomach churn. "No thank you. I believe I'll rest. My time may be coming."

"Oh, then do what's best. Maybe you should sleep in the spare room." George hated the idea of feminine bleeding, wombs, children, so it served as the perfect excuse.

"I will. I wouldn't want to disturb you. Good night." She kept her footfalls quiet, her anger confined, and still stepped out onto the terrace for a cigarillo before moving into the spare room. As she puffed clouds of smoke into the air, a plan took shape. No way would the asshole get away with his rudeness. In fact, she silently wished all men to the gates of hell before stubbing her smoke out and moving inside.

\*\*\*

Luther should've been in bed over an hour ago, but, instead, he found himself on a stroll toward the engineer's house. He'd half hoped to catch her outside, overlooking the night and smoking. Just as he liked to do in the evening. *Damn*. Giving into memories fell into a category of the worst things a man could do. He regretted the moment Janken had told him Eva was here. And the need he possessed to get her out. In the past, the woman proved she'd dig herself in and out of her messes, but the only way this plan would work was with her.

He circled the building, catching a glimpse of a lighted lamp through one of the kitchen windows. Stepping close to the wall, he inched along to take a peek. If he spotted anyone attempting sabotage, he'd bust in. Instead, his glimpse through the window revealed Eva at the table, piling slices of meat and cheese between two thick baguette pieces. He watched her eat, sipping milk or buttermilk from a glass. Truly, the Brit and Eva received over-the-top treatment in this house, with food selections not even offered to the soldiers.

Pampered and prissy, she'd gotten herself caught. Got herself all the trouble in the world, and she enjoyed the security the *bastardo* gave her. No sense in wasting his time. As she finished the last bite, he couldn't help tapping on the window twice. She jumped and coughed, eyes ablaze with curiosity. He pointed to the door and gestured for her to join him.

She left the lamp on the table and moved toward the back of the house. He followed, drawn like a moth to a flame, wanting to talk, the excuse his brain conjured up. Circling a couple of bushes, avoiding a couple of molehills, and finally, he stood at the servants' entrance to the home. She cracked open the door. "What are you doing here?"

"Wanted to make sure everything was safe here," he whispered, taking in the cream-colored silk robe— the one she'd worn the other day when he'd kissed her.

She moved outside, shut the door quietly, and stood on the top step, which brought her right in line with his face. "I'm surprised at why you had to do such a thing. It wouldn't have something to do with accusing George of not protecting me."

Her aggravated tone irked him. The *bastardo* didn't care about her, yet she offered her loyalty. "I heard he preferred to be called Herr Buckner. Formalities for the lowly people and such."

"I'm not lowly. I'm his consort."

Luther snorted. "He must be one hell of a lover to have earned your favor. Did you fuck him tonight?"

"We're not going to discuss my bedroom activities. In fact, it stopped being your business when you abandoned me in France."

Again, the past. She brought out the devil in him. "Too bad the magical spot between your legs couldn't keep me where you wanted me." He regretted the words as soon as they flew out of his mouth.

His cheek became the logical target for her slap, and he received it without complaint. Something becoming more common the more time he spent with her, why did her violence inflame him more? "Do you want to hit me again?"

"Not if you're going to enjoy it. Now, tell me why the hell you came up here?"

"He doesn't give a shit about you. The Brit. You're just some *mulatto* whore, a plaything, and he's having fun letting you prance around to do his bidding."

Her face scrunched at the evil word he hated so much. Hated how it affected how she perceived herself when the only things he ever associated her with came from her strength, bravery, and beauty. The parts of her he never wanted to see destroyed.

"I think you're jealous." She tugged at the edges of her robe in a futile attempt to cover herself and her exposed neck.

"Are you cold?"

"Quit changing the subject. I'm fine. Anything else?" The distant, icy woman he'd met a couple of years ago, when she'd asked for his help, returned in full force.

"Nothing, except to make sure you have a report ready in the morning to go out, and make sure *George* looks incompetent."

She chuckled, her voice low and smoky, like when she sang those Delta blues tunes. "If everything you say holds true, then he doesn't need my help. He's already an idiot." Turning away from him, she grabbed the handle of the doorknob and turned gently. After the door had opened without a squeak, he moved. She let go of her hold on the knob as he pulled her against him. The door stayed open.

He ran his free hand down her cheek, caressing the soft skin he remembered so well. "You're right. He is an idiot. You're not a plaything. No, *dea*. Beauty and pleasure are gifts sent to you by heaven. Never believe anything less."

The sigh she let loose before melting against him sent erotic images zipping around his brain like the electric currents streaking through a Tesla coil. He pushed her back to a standing position, turned on his heel, and got the hell out of there. He needed to keep his emotions squirreled away where she couldn't find out about them. Opening up to Eva or attempting to comfort her wouldn't get him anywhere but locked up.

# Chapter Five

A week had passed, and Eva still rode above it all, on the clouds. Since their late-night meeting, she'd turned over daily reports to Luther for the general field marshal, stayed demure and quiet in front of George, and played raging blues and jazz tunes during the day.

She still faked her menstrual to keep George at bay, but, each night, her dreams erupted with memories and new imaginings of her and Luther. He'd called her by the sweetheart nickname bestowed so many years prior, *dea*. *Goddess* in Italian, and a name he hadn't called her in years. The time he'd beat up those rich men for calling her *mulatto* pushed through her memories. He'd taken them on in Janken's club, beating them within an inch of their life, forcing them to kiss her feet, and she'd fallen for him, hard. Before then, she'd ignored his attentions, but he'd defended her honor because he disagreed that the color of her skin determined her worth.

The front door slammed open, and she jerked away from her piano, ready to verbally skewer whoever made the racket, expecting the man who put flutters in her belly and ridiculous dreams in her head. Instead, the visitor was, in truth, a most unwelcome one.

"Frau Sonne, so you're alive and well." The condescending voice along with the strands of white-ish blond hair combed over the top of his balding head scratched at her nerves. Not to be misjudged by his height, General Field Marshal Sauer could easily overpower a person. A body, though older, still well-hewn and muscled, had easily taken apart her personal hired muscle. She watched in horror as he'd snapped the man's wrist, then his elbow, and finally dislocated the stubborn fool's shoulder. Any resistance she'd possessed fell by the wayside afterwards. Add in his constantly present pair of bodyguards, as ruthless and as cold as the general himself, it'd be silly to think anyone stood a chance.

"A surprise visit. What did I do to deserve such an honor?" No sense in hiding her sarcasm. They could share in their dislike of one another. "I hope the trip out here didn't inconvenience you."

"Always a bitch. I hope you're not treating our Brit with a sarcastic mouth." He dropped his hat on top of the piano and proceeded to the shelf of decanters. All full, all the time. He poured himself a brandy while he spoke, without granting her a second glance. "I'm here because over a week ago your reports stopped arriving. When I reach out to the communications post, I'm told no one has delivered any letters from you and your guard died in an auto explosion in front of the chateau. Tell me how this stops your reports."

*Damn him.* She'd written a letter every day with information to make her engineer lover look more incompetent than a guard caught screwing on duty. He'd obviously kept them and laughed at her in the process. How much longer did she plan on letting men guide her life? Her fingers reached for the necklace she wore, a composition of magnetic genius and a gift from her mentor. No more games could be allowed, not with her safety.

"I apologize for the lack of communication, but, General, I feared anarchists are at work and aware of my reports. What better way to signal my distress without giving them more information about the tunnel? I'm familiar with the importance of this project, and downfalls would be as much mine as Herr Buckner's." The lies rolled off her tongue with ease.

"What makes you suspect such a thing?"

She turned back to the piano and lowered the cover over the keys, playtime over. "The fact they attacked the man who delivers my reports to communications and no one else. Herr Buckner's schedule and vehicle are easy to determine. The man behaves hopelessly British and keeps a punctuality the French do not envy. Likewise, my daily activities are not as predictable as his with the one exception of my guard leaving sometime during the day to take a note to communications. Also, there's no way to determine if Ka— if the soldier died before or after the explosion. No one watched him. None of the maids hard at work peeked out a window. Nothing."

Sauer nodded as he took little swallows from his drink. "It appears some of your white ancestry made you a bit smarter than I gave you credit for, and here I'd come to relieve you of your duty and end your non-loyal ways."

He'd never earn the pleasure of seeing the relief pulsing through her veins. She'd come to suspect his hatred for people of color and women in general, but seeing it point blank reminded her of the tightrope she'd started to traverse. "I thank you for providing the chance to explain. Can I get you any other refreshment?"

When playing the role of supplicant, always offer more than they could want—a rule she'd learned and followed well.

"No, Frau. Though, I will join Herr Buckner for dinner. Be sure to set an extra place and that you are not seated next to it." Grabbing his black visor cap and leaving the empty glass, he stalked out of the room, guards taking up position behind him. She wanted to stick her tongue out in protest, to call him a killer and much worse, but she held back like she'd done for so long.

No sooner did the door shut to the foyer than the one leading toward the dining room burst open. Luther marched in. "We should celebrate. It worked."

"You mean your plan to send my reports professing George's ignorance worked. When, in fact, you never sent them."

He shrugged and paused mid-step as the sound of a Jeep motor echoed off the house. When it got farther away, he continued, "I weighed the possibilities of the original plan against my own ideas and decided to try mine first. It looks like I achieved success, and, after seeing the bastard from outside my intelligence report bears truth, he's the one I'm going to kill."

The laugh bursting from her mouth started small but soon grew raucous. His withering, angry stare did nothing to calm her, either. After a few minutes, she got it under control enough to confess, "You say the funniest things. I honestly believed you were joking before. Now, I realize you're truly serious—"

"Why wouldn't I be?"

"Many have tried to kill him, and you see...he still lives." She threw her hands in the air. "Better to stick with whatever plans you have for blowing up the tunnel and get the hell out of here."

"How did you hear about the tunnel?"

"Why else would you come here? I sent those plans and maps to Janken to sell to someone who wanted to blow this damn monstrosity to kingdom come. Here you are. Except now you want to murder someone untouchable, and such a plan will get us all killed. There are plenty of ways to destroy the project, to make the channel tunnel fail dramatically. Adding premeditated murder would be a hell of a lot more difficult."

"My main reason for coming never involved the tunnel. The goal has always been Sauer, and I intend to kill him. If I get the other accomplished at the same time, then so be it. If not, no problem. My only other responsibility is to get you out of here."

"Excuse me?"

"Janken and his dear mama want you freed from this prison. One of your making, I'm sure of it now, but

I'm supposed to deliver you." He said the words sarcastically, as if he neither cared if he followed through or not. Like the German he so despised, he poured a glass of brandy. A popular choice for the day and she'd even admit to wanting a taste of it. Anything to dull a number of ridiculous notions filling the room.

"I'm not going back to New Orleans. The only good thing to come out of being dropped on French soil was the life I made for myself, a good one. I intend to get it back."

He threw back the sum of his glass, no nursing sips like the general. "Still pining away for the club the Germans took from you, I see. They won't return it, and, even if you go there, you won't own it."

"Maybe I should get married."

"A front?"

She stood and approached him. "What do you care? You'll be done with me, and I with you."

"Then, let the plotting begin."

Luther moved out of the piano room and into the parlor. Thankfully, Eva followed without argument, carrying her own glass of brandy. Was abandoning his original intentions of blowing the tunnel for a chance at Sauer premature? When he'd seen Sauer, it had taken everything inside of him to stop from launching through the window and pulling his knife. A waste of life, indeed. No, settling to plan, to develop a course of action seemed best. If Django failed to arrive in the time it took to execute this assassination, then they'd abandon the idea of stopping the tunnel. There remained a few possibilities of the project getting off the ground without Sauer.

"You speak of plotting, so plot." Eva plopped into one of the two high-backed chairs they'd occupied before. She wore the brown-and-pink dress she'd received the other day.

"Why do you insist on wearing such an awful dress?"

"Why do I think you're incapable of any real mercenary acts when you're always changing the subject to my clothing? I wear it to placate. Any good spy entrenched behind the enemy lines would do the same." She'd proven intelligent in times past, and this situation demonstrated it yet again.

Didn't mean he had to like the dress or her decision to appease her captor. He wanted her fiery and combative with the true enemy and not him. "Fine. I need to have access to Sauer and his guards.

81

I've got men in place with me here to assist with incapacitating them."

"How many men?"

"There are three of us." Telling the truth would leave him vulnerable, and he'd already exposed enough of his real motivations regarding his devotion to killing the General.

"It will take all of you, and you'll only get one chance."

"We must determine the appropriate time to take our chance. What's this about anarchists?"

She smirked. "Eavesdropping, the art of young children and men named Luther."

"And people who plan to be successful. Those glass windows are not good at blocking out things, either." He turned, focusing on the other objects in the room: the fireplace, the bookshelf, the small table at the end of the divan. The flowered wallpaper, faded and cracked. This house had endured years of mistreatment during the war, and even more now. When he turned back, she'd finished her drink. "The anarchists?"

"Yes, there are horrible rumors spread by peasants in this region about hidden groups who've taken to the woods and plot against German transports, projects, and laws as a way to fight against the occupation. I told Sauer the Jeep and Karl's death might have been planned by one of those groups. Our general has been a subject of many supposed anarchist threats and attempts, which may be the reason he became some sort of a legend among the military as one impossible to kill."

No sense in telling her the groups existed and the leader of one such group traveled toward the camp at Coquelles by now, carrying enough explosives to render the tunnel useless. If he didn't help the anarchists use it, Django would find a way. "Then let's use this rebellious band of people as a way to get to him. Feed him the intel you've uncovered, a plot against him, and lead him to the trouble. My men and I will accompany him and then turn on him once we've gotten him to the woods. It won't take much."

"Do you honestly believe this ridiculous plan will work?"

"I don't see why not. In strategy, working with a small group of soldiers has proven wiser than trying to organize a large force. Otherwise, you scare the enemy and send them into hiding. The guerilla tactics of such a group would put German soldiers at a disadvantage." The reasoning's came easily. He'd sold similar lies to half a dozen other people before. When facing an enemy, there always existed a way to defeat them. The challenge came in what lies to tell to hasten the defeat. He'd kill when necessary, but words did the majority of his work, unlike the previous leader of The Cursed.

"You actually sound believable. When do you want to do this?"

"You are more familiar with Sauer than I, so you're best suited to make the time determination. Of course, he won't stay here long, since finding you hearty and alive."

She absently stroked a section of her hair. It had grown longer since he'd seen her before coming to the camp, almost to her shoulders, but still solid sable...and the light reflected off it, reminding him of a night sky with stars twinkling. Foolish ideas.

Her gaze met his, and she snapped her fingers. "The kitchen servants live in Calais and travel between here and there. It would be easy to claim I overheard a couple of them talking about an attack."

"Right. As for the when, gauge his mood then make me aware. I want him off-guard, cocky, and maybe you can help influence that. I'll be here tomorrow as usual." The clock struck three in the afternoon, and a cuckoo sounded from the hall. "Annoying little thing."

"Fitting, I think, since we're about to do something insane. If this works, what happens then?" Her question was valid, but he didn't have a plan for after killing Sauer, yet.

His escape originally hinged on Django's arrival. They'd have to figure something else out. "I'll know more in the morning. Just plan on packing light. We can't carry all your clothing. Leave the ugly dress here."

\*\*\*

Eva smoothed the long sleeves of her thin midnight-blue dress. She still wore the magnetic necklace but had added her brooch bracelet, a weapon in disguise. If twisted the right way, an EMP could short circuit coil guns, electo wands, and other electric weapons. After her conversation with Luther and Sauer, she'd decided to take no more chances. Everyone needed to be viewed with distrust.

Tired of watching the men drink their alcohol in the parlor and debate the finer points on drill mechanics and treating her as an ornament rather than someone intelligent enough to join in the conversation, she'd finally excused herself and waited at the table for them to join her. Food had not been brought from the kitchen, yet, but the wine waited to be poured. She took the liberty of giving herself a full measure, versus the half or quarter-sized serving her narcissistic lover usually provided. It'd be easy enough to swallow half of it in one gulp, and she did.

A few moments later, George entered, followed by Sauer. The general's bodyguards took up position, one at the door and another in front of the dining room window directly behind her. The fool obviously didn't realize he'd be better off behind his boss than standing guard over a window no one dared to attack through. She should've asked Luther if he employed a sharpshooter in his band of rebels. They'd have better luck with a far off shot than attempting some close-range attack.

"Dear," George's voice broke her out of her musings. "Are you feeling all right?"

"Fine, why do you ask?" Another sip of wine, a polite smile, and she could get through this dinner.

"I called your name, asked you a question, and you appeared a little lost in in your own musings."

She chuckled. "I'm sorry. Lost in memories. One of the guards." Raising her hand, she pointed at the one stationed by the door. "He looks like Karl."

"Karl? The soldier in the Jeep?" George put a hand over hers. He sat at the head of the table as always. She didn't dare risk a glance at the general, for fear of giving away her mind's considerations.

Nodding, she reached for her handkerchief on the table and sniffled lightly.

"Do you want to go to bed?"

Sauer spoke before she could. "*Nein*. Frau Sonne must eat and not waste tears on a fool of a soldier. Obviously, he did not care about his life, or he would've taken his job more seriously."

The first course came and went. A potato soup concoction heavy with leeks, onions, and turnip. They called it potato soup only because the cook did. Potatoes grew best farther north in England and Ireland.

The conversation still centered on the tunnel and the machinery. When the second course arrived, the general poked and prodded the piece of cod, lightly fried in some cornmeal batter. If they'd only add some spices, Eva could almost believe herself at home, on the Delta.

She ate with gusto, asking between bites, "Is the cod not to your liking, Sir General?"

The gaze he leveled at her sent a chill down her spine, those beady black eyes on hers revealing something evil inside the man. "Cod is a dirty fish species, and the taste proves far too salty for me."

George, never believing in having anyone unhappy at his table, called for the cook. When she appeared, he demanded, "Take this away and bring the next dish. The general deserves food that makes him happy."

Braised beef came next, and where they got beef baffled her. Rich people owned the cows, and, last she'd checked, no one rich lived nearby. A few wealthy families in Calais may have had access to an occasional slab, but they wouldn't have shared with George. No matter, she ate slowly, enjoying each delicious piece as much as she could. The pair of fools kept talking business, but when talk turned to the workers, things got heated.

"I hear you're feeding the prisoners extra rations," the general remarked.

Selfish or not, her engineer suffered from problems with a weak workforce. "I can't afford to lose them, not with the drills going down every couple of days. I've already lost too many to illness and weak constitutions. Truly, hard labor keeps me on target. Working two crews, twelve-hour shifts so the construction never stops, and so, yes, rations have been increased. But no more have died."

"Did you ever consider we send them here to die?" The most ridiculous question asked with deadly calm.

Eyes on her plate, Eva didn't spare a glance to either of them, just sliced through another bite of steak and stuffed it in her mouth. *The best way to keep your mouth shut, keep it full.* Madame Le Roux said the same phrase often to all the girls in her establishment. Whether with food, drink, or cock, they kept their mouths full when verbal communication made them unhappy. The same tactic prevented her from calling Sauer out for being a monster.

George gave a sheepish shrug and took a sip of wine before replying, "No, I'd not considered the situation in such a fashion. Then perhaps we should be able to count on more regular replacements."

"Those dogs working for you are enemies of our country. Many are dissidents, thieves, rapists, or worse, the impure. Our nation won't flourish with those types wandering free or being punished with a slap on the hand. I'm afraid the kaiser learned long ago such behaviors can't be tortured out of them, and keeping them incarcerated only comes at the expense of the people, the hardworking individuals seeking to feed their families." Sauer paused, set his fork and knife down then reached for the bottle of wine and poured himself another glass. "I'm familiar with your soft heart, George, but these dogs take advantage of your giving nature. If they see weakness, they will exploit it. The best interests of both our governments lie in cutting the rations back down to the original levels. If their work productivity drops, cut it in half again. I'll get you more labor. Don't even hesitate to ask."

George, the fool, chewed on a giant piece of meat and nodded his agreement. A coward through and through. Such a man would never give her true security. As soon as her place at his side was challenged by the general or another like him, George would release her without hesitation. He cared more about himself and his supposed genius mind. A genius unable to figure out someone tampered with his drills by not oiling them properly and by adjusting the petrol mix.

"Now, Frau. Tell me what new songs you've learned," said Sauer, in between bites.

She flashed her teeth. "I've learned some Bach and a piece by Beethoven. A quite haunting man, you would agree?"

"Indeed. He wrote several pieces I'm fond of. Do you play those along with the Delta blues tunes you're so fond of?"

Another spy, perhaps a servant with an eager mouth had told him about the songs she'd been instructed to leave behind her. But since Luther's arrival, and George's careless words, she would never lock up those pieces of her again. "Indeed. Classical, Delta blues, jazz…. I love all varieties of music. Even some German folk songs I learned in Hamburg."

Sauer took another drink while his frown deepened his thick blond eyebrows, a complete contradiction to the blue of his eyes. "Seems you may need to practice more of our heritage through music rather than these mournful depressing tunes. Wouldn't you agree, Herr Buckner?

George coughed, dabbing at his mouth with his napkin. "Yes. It'd be good to hear more songs from your country."

"I'll have the sheet music sent immediately, then. And, upon my return in a few weeks, we can have a concert, *ja*?

She failed to respond because, in her mind, music should be played as one's spirit deemed it to be played, not forced or coerced. Herr Buckner spoke for her. "Eva would love to sing for everyone. I think it'd cheer the soldiers up as well. A great idea."

Another bite of beef and a slice of carrot, paired with a nod of agreement, and more silent chewing. Better to stay quiet than attempt to murder them all. Yet. The men went back to talking, excluding her the way she preferred and, she half-listened to the conversation, playing an internal rendition of several songs, from Robert Johnson to Fred Astaire. The lyrics helped her keep a level head through the rest of dinner. When coffee finally reached the table, along with slices of an apple strudel Eva had smelled baking through the better part of the afternoon, she'd moved on to folk melodies learned from her French employees at the club. She ate every last morsel of flaky pastry and tender, melting apples.

After the endless evening, she parted her lips to excuse herself, but Sauer threw his napkin on the table and announced, "A fine dinner. I'll need to return to camp. A soldier proves his worth by living in the same conditions as his fellows. I'd appreciate Frau Sonne's escort to the front door."

*Merde*. The last thing she wanted to do, ever. Better to get this over with instead of listening to more demeaning ridicule the next day. If he wanted to get rid of her, then so be it. The last supper proved delicious enough to feed her hunger and imagination for weeks.

"I'd be honored, General." Eva pushed her seat back and waited for Sauer at the head of the table. He refrained from touching, and his disdain spiked her ire enough she wanted to force contact, just to watch him react. But she'd pushed this devil enough for tonight.

They walked side by side to the front door. Then, in the foyer, he turned on her, his menacing bodyguards taking up a position from behind. No running, no escape. She'd face her punishment now.

"A little bird tells me these anarchists you speak of may also be your friends. I'd like to believe they are threatening you in some way, possibly trying to kill foolish Buckner. Tell me truthfully, Frau."

She growled. "Rumors are nasty and not at all reliable. I'd think you'd have learned such things by now. As for my loyalty, why question it?"

"You've started playing music you've been forbidden to play. You wear tasteless colorful flowered frocks and prance around like a *hure*." He'd stepped forward midway through his little rant, spittle hitting her face when he called her a whore.

"The reason why I am here, remember? Except, instead of getting paid, I'm selling myself for free."

Sauer stepped back, focusing on the floor. He took a deep breath, and, when he raised his head, the angry red-faced man had disappeared. A coldhearted bastard took his place. "No, you're selling yourself to prevent a decaying two-story building from being smashed to rubble and the people living in it sent to work camps much like this one."

He produced two white envelopes from the inner pocket of his coat. "These arrived for you in Hamburg, after your departure. After I had them checked for any possible hidden messages, I believed it best if you received these. From your friends, of course. They are concerned about your return. If I stood in your shoes, I'd use this night to think on their words, Frau. Your friends would like you back, and I'm sure you want to keep them safe."

The *cul* said no more but left with bodyguards in tow. She clutched the envelopes, crinkling the paper within her fist. Additional words weren't needed. He'd renewed his threats and reminded her how a deal with the devil meant she'd well and truly fucked herself.

Her eyes had leaked too many tears. Wasted water, Janken's Voodoo mama called them, a sure way to fall prey to the heat in any season in the Delta.

She escaped upstairs, setting the letters aside until she'd swaddled herself in the silk nightgown, matching robe, and slippers. Then she tucked her feet up under her body, in the burgundy cloth high-backed chair in the guest room. Rather than switching on a lamp, she lit a fire to ward off the chill the breeze brought in from the coast. The flicking light gave off enough illumination to read Carmela's first letter. Dated over three months ago, her first contact from people she cared about mentioned the birth of the baby, the boys finding work, and everyone still holding on even after almost two years of being away. One of the girls, Rose, had run off with a German soldier who'd promised her marriage and a better life, only someone found her lifeless body in a forest a few days later.

A sob came out unbidden at the memory of beautiful Rose, a fine singer, and dancer. Eva had hoped to train her in stage performance upon her return, but she'd fallen to the German oppression. Another victim of false promises and a man's charms. She swiped at her eyes, rubbing them fiercely as if it would stop any more tears from forming. Crumpling the letter, she threw it into the fire, letting the flames act as her vengeance.

Unfortunately, the second letter contained bad news about the two young men who'd reached adulthood working for the club as stable boys, house boys, and eventually security for everyone who lived there. One of them, Henri, gave into the lure of the army, leaving behind his responsibilities for a career and the promise of steady quantities of food. Carmela told of how he'd vowed to send food back to them, or at least his earnings, when he'd left a month prior, but they'd received nothing from him since. Paulo, the other one, had fallen ill with a chill and sat near death's door. Her friend wrote hoping Eva would send money or medicine to them. Of course the letter was dated two months prior, and it was far too late for her to make a difference.

She tossed this one in the fire, too. What more could the general do, except kill the rest? Carmela and the baby, the other girls, and Paulo, if he'd survived. There would be no chance to save them unless she got rid of the threat. She calculated the options. Her choices were limited to the devil she knew or the one who'd trapped her.

*Damn.*

# Chapter Six

Luther arrived at the house ready to finalize their plan. The absence of Eva's music as he entered the foyer threw him. For the last week, she'd played a variety of tunes each morning, without fail. Today, the house lay in silence except for the comings and goings of servants. He put a hand on his knife hilt.

"*Wo ist die dame*?" he quizzed one of the women dusting around the cuckoo clock on the wall.

She pointed to the closed parlor doors and turned away. A strange group, these French servants who spoke little German but understood it well enough. He marched into the room, aware he could be interrupting a conversation between her and someone else, even Sauer. All the better for him to size the man up, potentially take him out today and be done with it. Instead, she sat alone, sipping an au lait.

No grin, no sassy remarks. In fact, everything around her had dimmed.

"Are you well?" he asked as soon as he'd shut the door.

"As well as I can be."

"Then where do we stand, are we—"

Eva drew a finger to her lips and then moved her other hand around in a circle. Someone listened to their conversations, and this beautiful woman had figured it out.

He moved closer to her, wanting to grab her circling hand and kiss it. So he did. Her breath hitched as his lips touched her smooth skin. Always soft, the color of the coffee she loved to drink. They'd have time enough to get a little more personal after he eliminated Sauer.

Pulling her hand out of his embrace, she picked up two letters from the small table and held them out. "These are ready for the post."

"I will get them to the communications center. Will you need anything else?"

She maintained a stiff and businesslike appearance. There could have been people watching and he'd nearly blown her cover. If questioned, he'd admit she tempted him beyond reason.

"No. Just get those letters delivered immediately." She went back to sipping her coffee and reading some book. Perfectly boring and an excellent way to throw off a spy.

"As the *dame* demands." He bowed and left the room, letters secure in his pocket. Since the accident, he'd kept with walking, multiple times a day, to and from the camp. For exercise and because it allowed him to see things he'd otherwise miss like two soldiers sneaking away for a quick screw in the woods or Sauer's bodyguards searching tents. *Interesting*.

Going the long way around, he passed the communications tent and headed for his own. Hans slept deeply, and Arik lay with his eyes closed, his shift started later than usual today. Sitting down on his bed, he read the first note. A bunch of friendly, touchy-feely platitudes to some woman named Carmela in a town to the south, the location for Eva's club. He folded it back up and decided to take it on to the post. The first communication she'd ever given him to take to a friend, and there seemed no reason to withhold it.

The second letter possessed the information he wanted, addressed to Sauer, which he found odd since the general had already arrived in camp. The irony was, when he opened the note, it read to him and not the asinine man he planned to kill.

*Luther,*

*I've convinced Sauer the anarchists will attempt to attack the camp tonight. He plans to ambush them at the little church on the back half of the chateau property around ten. Be in the woods behind the church and you can catch him and his bodyguards inside. This will be the only shot we have. I've discovered a spy in the house and cannot speak of these details so do not return to the house today.*

*I'll meet you at the church around midnight, and from there we can escape.*

*Eva*

She'd come through. His spirit buoyed at the prospect of finally getting revenge against the man who'd ripped him from his childhood. The man who would've sold his sister to the Americans, promising freedom only if she killed the president and his son. Such a feat would've resulted in capture and certain death. Now, he'd be able to stop the general's other plots, though not taking down the tunnel bothered him a bit.

"Arik."

"Yes?"

"Get word to Dietrich. Tonight we take out Sauer, his bodyguards, and whoever reports with him. Meet me here in the tent after dinner. We'll gather our gear and head to the church." He lit a match and set fire to Eva's letter. No chances could be taken from this point on. They needed to be successful. Maybe he could come back or leave Hans in place to finish off the tunnel once Django arrived.

"What about ol' prisoner guard over there?" They'd taken to giving Hans a hard time because his job seemed to be the easiest. Guarding dead tired and barely-able-to-keep-upright prisoners proved not much of a challenge.

"He'll stay at his post. Can't raise any suspicions tonight. At the most, there will be ten men. We've got electo wands between us, a couple of EMP grenades, and we can always smoke them out. Can either you or Dietrich get ahold of a coil rifle?"

Arik shrugged. "Not sure, but I'll pass the word on before I head to my shift. We should be able to get something."

Nothing for it. They'd get what they could and attack. All of his men had intimate experience on how to kill with their bare hands. Knives would do well in this situation, too. "Get what you can, and we'll make do. Until tonight."

\*\*\*

Eva hid under the bushes on top of a small hill opposite the little church. Behind her, the chateau loomed, lights blazing, but she waited and watched. Sauer and his men took up position inside the decaying brick building. No lanterns or candles. They'd gone in armed and lay in wait for the anarchists.

She had no clue if Luther and his men had already gathered at their rendezvous spot since she'd stayed behind in the house until the general's crew headed out. Only then had she followed to watch and see how everything went. In the end, she'd spent most of the evening not trying to feel guilty for lives about to be lost. While she played tough and even defended herself once or twice, killing, in any form, did not top the list of things she enjoyed.

Often, too many lives were lost without cause. Her decisions were based on the best chance of survival, the best chance of getting out of this with the people she cared about alive and well.

Her wayward musings halted at three shadows moving out of the trees and toward the church, illuminated by the moonlight and visible thanks to her binoculars. Stealth and hand signals seemed their only form of communication.

The front doors to the one towered abandoned place of worship burst open as they reached the entrance, and Sauer's men filed out, calling for Luther and his group to halt. A smoke grenade launched through the air, and laser fire broke out. Several coil guns whipped strands of purplish-blue through the air. Shouts rang out, the cries of men in pain, and when the smoke cleared, Luther and one of his men sat in custody. The third man lay clutching his chest, and writhing on the ground. He appeared younger than the others, and Sauer said something, then approached him and touched an electo wand to his head. The contact sent the young man's body twitching and smoking until he went still. She didn't miss the grin on the general's face, nor did she ignore the punch to the gut she received in reaction. One life for many was the only justification she'd allow herself.

Standing up, she let the binoculars hang loose and hit the center of her chest, relishing the pain, making it a part of her and accepting it as punishment. Then she trudged back to the house, her boots snagging on rocks, head cast downward. Finally, she sat on the steps of the servants' entrance and waited.

The soldiers' celebration as they dragged Luther and his surviving comrade over the hill and down to the house became loud enough to bring George outside.

She glanced up at his confused face. "Good evening."

"What's going on? I was readying for bed, and a loud commotion started up."

"Yes, the general has caught anarchists." A grand accomplishment, most likely earning the *cul* another medal or some such nonsense.

"There's no such thing. Probably just some boys.... No, wait. They have the soldier who confronted me, the one assigned to guard you." George's hands raked through his hair, and he glanced down at his body as if checking for injury. "The man could've tried to kill me. To ruin the tunnel."

"Or set fire to your precious books."

"Indeed," her idiotic lover agreed. Not once did he mention her nor even ask what role she'd played. She'd cast herself in the role of betrayer, and Luther's deadly, cold stare told her as much.

"It appears your information was correct, Frau Sonne." Sauer stopped in front of her and sneered, a big grin overtaking his already less-than-appealing features. "We've got the dissidents who tried to threaten you and get you to agree to their demands."

"Eva?" George looked even more confused. "They threatened to hurt you?"

"Yes, they threatened all manner of horrible things, including torturing you, darling. I couldn't let such an awful thing happen, so, this morning, I told the general everything, and we devised a plan. It worked." Her confession revealed the reality. She'd chosen the devil who possessed the ability to save everyone she loved. Luther couldn't promise her such things. In fact, he'd promised her help years prior and delivered nothing. No, pure pain and further heartache came from the man who'd once loved her body so well.

"Well, thank heavens you did. I'm amazed at your courage and strength." George leaned down and wrapped his hands around her shoulders, squeezing gently—odd way of giving comfort, the one emotion she didn't want.

Nothing could assuage her guilt as her ex's hatred blazed forth, pinning her in place until the general spoke. "Yes, indeed. She showed good will to Germany and England. Very fortuitous."

"What will be done with the captives?" She had to ask, had to know.

Sauer eyed her, and his words echoed with a warning. "They'll be interrogated, thoroughly, by me. I must see if any other plans may be in the works to threaten this or other projects of the empire. If we find any other anarchists, the same thing will happen."

"Right, indeed," George said. "Inform us if there's anything else we should be concerned with. Come, Eva. Let's go to bed."

She stood, at her lover's suggestion, and allowed him to usher her inside. He escorted her to the guest room, giving her a chance for another night apart. His mention of how the evening's events shook her up came as a complete surprise, and he droned on for a few minutes before closing the door behind him.

Numb, she wandered aimlessly toward the bed, leaving her boots, coat, and all clothes in place. Exhaustion took over before the nightmares could come.

***

The next morning, she pulled her hair back in a tight bun, donned black trousers, a white blouse, and boots. Downstairs, she met the general and George for breakfast. They briefly discussed drills and an arriving train, but she could care less about such things. In fact, if Sauer delivered, she'd be packing after breakfast.

Toast, a cup of coffee, and George left to play at digging a hole in the ocean. She, on the other hand, waited to be acknowledged.

"You seem tired, Frau. Did sleep not come to you?"

"I slept very much like the dead. Probably why I appear that way. Now, you have your anarchists. When can I expect to leave? You'd mentioned as early as today—"

"I'm afraid that's impossible." He shook his head slowly with his words. "George has expressed that he can't continue his work without you. Your presence grants him peace, calm, and a sense of safety. Especially since last night."

She'd never listened to so much horse shit. "You're a horrible liar. The man can barely see past his own demented, selfish ways to care whether I'm here or not. We had a deal."

"Deal? I've amended back to our original agreement." He pushed out of his chair, throwing the napkin he'd used moments ago to dab his cheeks with to the table. "I'm for Berlin. The kaiser has requested my presence. I'll return within the week, and we may be able to discuss your situation further. Maybe some aid to those you feel responsible for, your special band of whores and unwanted orphans. *Auf wiedersehen, Frau* Sonne."

After he had left the room, she hurled the coffee cup at the closest wall. It shattered, spraying tan colored café au lait on everything in the cup's path. She didn't care who reported it to the damn man or if he listened to her cry of anguish mixing in with the noise. Her efforts amounted to nothing. She'd never be released from this prison, and only gained the possibility of food, clothing, and maybe medical supplies—a long shot on the medical piece. Even those promises couldn't be trusted since they monitored all her communications, and if Carmela wrote about the lack of help or very little assistance, she'd never receive the letter.

She struggled out of the dining room and into the piano room, tears leaking from her eyes. Sitting on the piano bench, she placed her hands on the piano keys. Trembling, she played a song of mourning. The wailing sounds of Robert Johnson and his haunting words about the devil, hell hounds, and selling one's soul fit her mood for the day. She'd gambled and lost, chosen the wrong horse. Janken's mama often told stories of those who'd sought a variety of things from freedom to fortune. Those stories always ended badly, and it appeared hers would, too.

So, she played. Played for the people she loved, the ones she'd lost, and the ones she'd abandoned. As the music cleansed her mind, her soul searched for clarity. Each new tune brought her closer to figuring out the next path to take and, unfortunately, this path involved talking to the one man who probably wanted nothing to do with her. The trick would be to figure out how to get Luther to trust her again.

# Chapter Seven

A brand new day required a revised plan. She'd go into the soldier's camp and see Luther. Possibly under the ruse he'd stolen something of hers, and she wanted it back. A piece of jewelry or a letter.

*Hell.* She shut the front door and stomped her foot. How could she discover Luther's location, meet with him, and keep news of her actions from George? Altogether, her spying skills could be chalked up as poor since she kept herself so far away from everything. Waiting around for things to happen had never been her style, part of the reason she'd ended up here.

Marching down the dirt road to the camp, she hummed an old tune, some little ditty about dust and thirst. When a couple of soldiers, patrolling the path inquired as to her direction, she told them she'd decided to take a stroll. They shrugged and let her continue. At least Sauer hadn't spread the word of her being a threat. No, the pompous *cul* believed her to be a suitably subdued and controlled worker bee. Too bad she planned to prove him wrong. Double-crossers deserved what they got.

She paused at the top of the hill, staring down into a sea of tents, some larger than others. On the far side lay a building, most likely housing the machines. To her right, barbed fences surrounded several rows of tents, prisoners' quarters. She'd try there first. Maybe a soldier could be bribed with a kiss. They deprived these men of female companionship for months at a time.

And the regard they gave her as she passed into the rows of tents displayed the deprivation. Hungry stares reminding her of ravenous dogs contributed to the goose bumps popping up on her arms. Her hair stood up at the back of her neck as she briskly moved past them. Even with the trousers, blouse, trench coat, hat, and boots she wore, they still recognized as her prey. They perceived her as weak because she was female, but she'd never be caught in a situation without protection. She tucked both hands into her coat pockets, slipping fingers into the electo knucks inside. A small press of a button, and the iron would buzz with current. The rubber padding lining the rings protected her from the electric shock, but anyone else would get a face full.

She moved to the right, heading for the prisoners' area. Ducking between tents, keeping a straight line, and then dashing through the middle into another row, she became a moving target. Someone followed her, rising hairs on the back of her neck a telltale sign, and then a hand circled her waist, locking her arms against her body. Another hand slapped over her mouth before she could let out a scream.

Tent flaps gave way as they backed up. The flaps closed, cutting them off from anyone who might help, and she wiggled like a fish caught between a fisherman's hands. The effort did nothing.

Finally, her captor said, "*Madame, calme.*"

French words in a deep manly voice, possibly a trick to make her feel safe. The best way to get her arms free was following instructions. So she quit struggling, and he put her feet on the ground then he let go.

She turned to face the idiot, whipping her arms free from the coat and pressing the buttons on the bottom of the knucks with her thumbs. The waking current put a hum in the air, and she let a fist fly, connecting with her captor's cheek.

He went down immediately and pleaded, "*Dame Eva, la pitie.*"

Only a few people called her by the honorific of lady, which had been a gift from her mentor. The employees of her club had continued the tradition.

She turned the knucks off and reached out a hand. "Stand. Any tricks, and there's more punishment for you."

"*Oui, madame.*" A tanned hand, matching her own, clasped hers and she stood firm as he used her weight to pull himself to his feet. "Don't you remember me? Henri?" His English sounded stilted, but when she'd left he'd still been learning, on top of the German everyone was forced to become familiar with. The hazel eyes, the black hair with the slight curl, and the skin, which never burned in the sun, only got darker. He'd never gained much height, standing only a foot or so above her, but he'd filled out his body a bit. Seduced into the military, he'd been the one who ran away.

"Henri…. Yes, I do remember. Why did you leave everyone?"

"To help them, of course, but these Germans lie. They say we can write to our families, but no responses are ever received. They tell us food will be given as part of our payment, but I have no way of discovering if Carmela and the others have gotten anything. And then you're here in the rows of the camp. My heart rejoiced."

She patted his shoulder. "Yes, I'm happy to see you, too."

He'd always been a bit dramatic, and now proved no exception. "But why are you endangering yourself. The men here they—what's the word, lust? Yes, they lust after women. They talk about what they will do when they get one. Very dangerous here."

They'd worked at a club just as hazardous. She'd spent every night armed, as he had. "The world is dangerous, Henri. I'm here because I have to find a man."

"You found me." He struck a soldier's pose, hand raised in salute and back ramrod straight.

"Yes, thankfully, I did. But I'm seeking a man who's been captured. He posed as a lieutenant and had another soldier imprisoned with him."

"They brought two men into the building where they keep the machines. I listened to them speaking about separating them from the others."

Eva put her knucks back in their respective pockets. "Perfect. Can you take me there?"

Henri shook his head and frowned. "No, the way's unsafe, and we'll be caught."

"I've got to talk to him. He's my only hope of getting out of here."

"Are you captive?" The boy-turned-man reached out and touched her arm, sympathy shining in those eyes. "It would explain why you didn't come back."

Finally, someone she could apologize to. "I'm so sorry, Henri. I wanted to, but they caught me and forced me here." No sense in trying to explain how she'd been spying for Luther on the false promise he'd help her get her home back. She'd probably never get it back, but not owning the building could be overcome if she could get home.

"No apology, *Dame* Eva. We worried, for sure." He paused, gripping her arm tight. A group of men stomped by outside, talking loudly about finding the woman. She reached into her pocket again but stopped as the soldiers moved on. "This tent's not a safe place for you, either. Let me take you back."

"I can't. Not without seeing the lieutenant."

"I take you home, and you see him tomorrow." Henri's gaze told her he believed the words he said.

"How?"

"There's a way. I will find a way." He wouldn't elaborate any more, and she finally agreed. One more day, one more night spent in restless sleep trying to figure out a way to escape.

\*\*\*

One word described Luther's current state: thirsty. They'd deprived them of food and drink for the last forty-eight hours. He wanted water. Any type would do, but a beverage would moisten his cracked lips. Dietrich didn't fare much better, and the worn-out soldier with mud and blood caked in his hair slept.

Luther hadn't experienced the same exhaustion. No, his mind replayed the images of the ambush, of Arik falling and then Sauer killing him with the electo wand. His heart pounded, chest ached as he'd been rendered helpless and able to do nothing.

He also recalled Eva sitting on the steps, eyes haunted by what she'd seen. Watching as a man died because she'd betrayed him or she'd been caught. He still didn't know for sure, except his gut told him she'd turned on them. He should've expected a double cross, since she'd chosen to come here and give away a part of herself merely to survive. Her motivations confused him because his way meant freedom. She'd picked the cage.

A knock sounded on the door of the closet they currently occupied. Other prisoners had been in here before, too. Dried blood stains and fingernail scratches proved repetitive occupancy. The hinges creaked as the door opened, and in popped Hans with his ridiculous glasses. "Captain?"

"I'm here, and don't call me captain." Luther's voice sounded awful, throating aching due to dryness.

"Right, Lieutenant." He opened the door and stepped inside. A shorter, youthful man followed him in, turning to face away from them and take guard.

"Who's with you?"

"His name's, Henri. He says Frau Sonne came searching for you yesterday. She wants to meet with you."

*Really*? "Does it mean water?"

"We can get you some." Hans motioned to Henri, and the youth freed his water bottle from his belt and tossed it over. An open cap and then his crewman kneeled before him pouring the liquid into his mouth. Refreshing and quenching, yes. The water soothed his throat but was gone way too soon.

Hans capped the bottle and tossed it back to Henri. Then he put both hands under Luther's armpits and brought him to a standing position. "We're going to say you're going for interrogation. No one can verify who's supposed to interrogate you. I've asked. We're going to a guard shack on the far side of the train platform, but I've got to leave the chains on until we get there."

Luther nodded. They left Dietrich sleeping. When Hans and the youth brought him back, he'd bring water for their comrade as well. The walk through the camp came with almost no attention. The Germans caring so little for why someone got escorted in chains spoke volumes toward their view of such treatment. Obviously, it was more commonplace than he'd expected. When they finally reached the shack, Hans came inside with him.

Eva jumped up from her chair at his arrival. She spoke no words, but her eyes said enough. He appeared awful no doubt. The chains fell to the floor, and he rubbed his wrists, enjoying the tingling sensation coursing through his fingers as feeling came back.

She watched the ankle locks get released then stepped forward. "I've brought food, water, and a wash basin if you want to clean up."

Luther nodded at Hans, and the man left. A peek showed him taking up position outside the door. "How long do we have?"

"All afternoon. No one uses this post, at least not unless a train comes in. There's one expected to arrive tomorrow, according to Henri."

He wanted to call her out, to yell and maybe even rage a bit, but found himself too exhausted. Instead, he settled for hobbling over to the basin set on a small table against the wall near the door. He poured cold, clean water over his head. Rivulets dripped off him and pooled in the bowl below. Dirt and blood discolored the water. Grabbing a bar of soap he scrubbed his face. Then he removed the shirt and cleansed his chest, arms, and neck. The sense of washing away the grime, and getting clean was a balm on his meager existence. His trousers went next, and he proceeded to wash his entire body. He dunked a towel in water and wiped off the soap suds, making a small mess on the floor. The worst part would be putting on the clothes again, making himself dirty once more.

When he turned to Eva, he lit up. She watched, mouth hanging open and amber eyes wide.

"Any clean clothes by any chance?"

"Uh...." She licked her lips, and he remembered the kiss from weeks ago. Her lips were soft then.

He should've been enraged. Yet, almost losing his life had changed his perspective. One more time wouldn't hurt, to hold her, to experience her body against his again. "Come here."

For once, she didn't fight but moved forward, and, when she stood a foot away, he pulled her flush against his wet body. She gasped, and he took advantage of her surprise and kissed her, hard, and then moved in with his tongue. She tasted sweet, with a hint of coffee. Yes, she'd been drinking café au lait not too long before they'd met. A moan, he had no clue if it came from her or him, but the original hunger in his belly transformed into something entirely different.

Cock hard, he wanted her now. "Tell me I can have you."

"Have me, please." Her words came out harsh against his lips.

He moved to her throat, pressing kisses, and she undid the buttons on her blouse, opening herself up to him. When he reached her collarbone, he sucked her skin, determined to mark her in some way. Her hands wormed their way between their bodies, releasing buttons and pushing the fabric keeping her skin from his out of the way. She wore a bra, a new fancy contraption he did away with, along with the blouse.

"One moment," she cried.

He pulled back, and she removed her boots and stepped out of her trousers. She stood there, buck naked, clothes mingling with the small puddle of water on the floor. Her hair fell over her, exposing the column of her neck and the perfect curvature of her spine. He was lost.

She leaned up and bit her bottom lip, a lustful look in her eyes. "All ready."

"I'll decide when you are," he growled and picked her up off the floor. Stalking to the desk, he spread her out on the bare surface. The wood wouldn't be comfortable, but it'd have to do. "Are you okay?"

"Fine. I need you."

He traced the curve of both breasts, then her nipples, their pale pink in complete juxtaposition to the rest of her coloring. He brought one into his mouth, pinching it between his teeth, and she groaned. Her hips bucked upward. How easy it'd be to bury himself inside her now. He struggled for control, wanting, no, needing, to pleasure her first. To taste her again and remind her of what she'd given up. What she'd lost in the betrayal she'd delivered.

Luther moved slowly down her body, caressing and kneading as he went, a determined expression on his face, focused, predatory. She damn near yelled out at him to hurry up. He drove her crazy, pure madness. She'd never meant for this to happen. The original goal had involved talking, but then he'd stood there naked, his erection like a proud flag, standing at attention, and he'd called to her. She'd melted against the desire for another chance to be in his arms, to experience the pleasure he'd offered to her many years before.

He spread her legs and put his tongue to her. She nearly cried out but stifled the noise by biting on her knuckle. No sense in alarming their guards. They probably comprehended what took place anyway, but brain function fled as his tongue flicked the small nub at the top of her womanhood. She didn't recall the names of the parts he touched, only how what he did to her stoked an inner fire, like a slowly building crescendo in some musical masterpiece.

Slowly, he pushed one finger into her, then two, and his ministrations with his wonderful, talented mouth didn't stop. He refused to quit when she begged him to. Her legs tensed, then a shiver ran up her spine, and when he put his tongue in the same spot as his fingers, she exploded. Her hand failed to reach her mouth in time to stop the high-pitched cry she let out.

Then he stood and, in one swift motion, thrust his cock into her. He set a pace similar to how his fingers performed, fast and relentless. She'd started to climb a new peak, this time at a quicker pace.

He met her pleas for more by pounding into her with such ferocity the desk beneath them creaked and rattled in protest. They'd probably break it, but she lost the sense to care. She wanted to enjoy him for as long as possible, to take him over the precipice he'd shoved her over minutes prior. He lifted her legs to his shoulders and kept up the brutalizing pace until a flash of light burst in her eyes like stars and he called out her name. He put her legs down and disentangled himself from the rest of her body.

She found the strength to point to a shelf behind him. "There's a clean worker's uniform on top. Henri helped get them for me."

Turning away, he went for the clothes, thankful for Henri, who brought him drawers and an undershirt as well. For someone who he'd believed wanted him dead, she showed an awful lot of concern. He shrugged his way into the uniform, and when he faced her again, she stood next to the desk.

A sheepish little half-grin formed on her face replaced quickly with a frown. "I'm sorry, for Sauer, giving away your position...everything."

"Why?" The question came out a bit rougher than he'd intended.

"Because I made the wrong move, but he left me no choice. He said he planned to take you captive, not kill you. I told him you were anarchists, not members of The Cursed. If you confess, he might show leniency, and you could get out."

She'd lost it if she believed he'd ever confess to being something he wasn't. Not his way, and, after what happened to Arik, he'd kill the bastard for sure. He pounded a fist against his chest to rid himself of the tight ache forming at thinking Arik's name.

"You've gone daft. Did they brainwash you or something? I'm not going to confess to anything."

"But he'll kill you."

"Not if I kill him first."

Her face flushed, eyes blazing. Time to tell the whole story. "Years ago. I was ten or so. My sister snuck outside our house to explore and got captured by a member of The Cursed. They had info about her, knew she'd been employed by the kaiser, and they sent a ransom to my parents." He blew out a breath to calm himself. He'd never spoken about this to anyone, but suffered in silence. "Sauer arrived after the kidnapping report had been filed. Of course, they all blamed me. My job was to guard her, shield her from harm, and I'd failed. I'd do anything to get her back, and the jackass general asked me to go to the drop site with a bag. Imagine, a young man, no clue what's in a big, leather sack, willing to make the drop for his sister."

Her angry face softened, and she whispered, "Were you scared?"

"Hell, yes. I'd never been so scared in my life. It got worse when they took me and the bag. I became part of the trade, along with a million francs worth of gold and jewelry. A healthy young boy because the captain had a soft spot for them." He let those words sink in, and the memories came back. The kindness shown him, the way Captain Bolga tried to get him to believe his family wanted nothing to do with him, and finally the inappropriate contact. Luther shuddered and shoved the images aside.

"They hurt you."

"The bastards tried, but they got fists and my training instead. You remember Bolga?"

"Yes." She nodded. "He liked to partake of Janken's buffet selection."

"I gave him the scar trailing from his forehead to his chin, with pleasure and a smile. He never tried to touch me again. No, instead he put me with another group of young ruffians and had me train them." The Cursed leader had turned his sights on more gullible prey, and he'd been too young to stop him. "It took me fifteen years before I could rally enough of the group to stand against him. He met the end of my blade in a fair fight. If not me, it would've been others. Arik suffered at his hands, too. We survived together. So forgive me if you think I'll settle for running away like a coward while the man who sent me to the monster of my past lives."

"I'm only asking you to do this because—" She stopped short, and he wanted to comprehend, ached to understand her.

"Tell me. If you do one thing, be truthful. I've had enough lies for the time being."

"I don't want to deal with more death. Sauer interrogated me after I got captured at the embassy. He found out about my club, about the people who worked there. Those same individuals who live there, I supported them from Hamburg. Selling baubles received from admirers or convincing men to give me extra money, which I used to get supplies to them. I never told them who I spied for, merely I'd come to gather information in the hopes of trading the information for help."

He found it hard to believe she'd kept his name out of it. "You never mentioned me."

The desk chair scraped on the floor as she pulled it out and sat down. "Why would I? They asked where your sister got off to. I told them north to the island, nothing else. The general found out he could use my people against me to get what he wanted, a spy in the house of a British engineer. See, I'd already found my way onto Sauer's list. If I'd stayed hidden, or not, failed to matter. George had already told anyone and everyone how much he admired me, wanted me. My days were hopelessly numbered before our friend would've recruited me. The capture made his job easier."

"So, you're here because of threats made to your employees, your gang?" He slipped his feet into the rubber-and-canvas blend slip-ons they gave all prisoners. "No luck getting my boots in here?"

She ignored his joke about the footwear and headed right back into argument territory. "They aren't a gang. They are women, young men, children, and babies with no place to go. No abilities outside what they already do, and I swore I'd keep them safe. Exactly why I came to you three years ago, and you, in a rather rude way told me to, and I quote, 'Spy for me on the side, and maybe we can work some things out.'"

Nothing prepared him for her little speech. Nothing at all. He'd been uncaring toward her situation back then, still trying to grasp his new position as a leader and get his plans in place. His duties made him responsible for a lot of folks, too. He'd never believed she cared more about other people than herself. She'd always watched out for her well-being before others. One of the reasons he'd never worried about her when he left her in France.

He spoke in a low, steady tone. "I won't apologize for my decisions back then, and I believed your excuses to be a ruse. How many lies had I heard from people wanting my help since I took command? I'm still not capable of making these things you want happen. My abilities are limited. My plan involved putting you in a safe place, a place you'd survive in, and then helping you when I could."

A laughed bubbled forth from her lips, loud and forced, before dropping off abruptly. "If it works once, do it again. Your plan didn't work either time, though. You didn't take into consideration those Nuremberg laws making it illegal for someone African, Jewish, or female to own property. Nor did you plan on foolish engineers admiring me or your bounty hunter and sister seeking me out." She stood, throwing her hands up in the air. "You say you ran with a plan, but the damn idea did little for me. Now you show up out of nowhere asking for me to trust you, believe you'll rescue me when all you're good for is a screw and getting the hell out."

He closed the gap between them and slammed his hand on the desk. "You're right."

Funny how she'd cut straight to the heart of their issues and the sins of the past leading them here. He'd done the very things she accused him of, and he had no defense.

"This time, I will make things right. I'm not leaving without fixing things."

Eva's shoulder's sagged, and she shook her head. "I don't see how. There's nothing here. I can arrange to have you snuck out on the next train."

"No." He grabbed one of her hands and laced their fingers together. "No way I'm leaving again. You don't want to face any more death, and I'm not going to let you stand against this shit storm by yourself. Besides, there's another plan in place, and I mean to see it through."

# Chapter Eight

Eva wrestled with the little devil inside her wanting to jump up and yell at Luther again. He believed she talked crazy, but trusting him continued to prove harder than she'd expected. "Not another plan. I can't deal with any more." She started to move around, wrestling her clothes back onto her body.

"I'm not talking about a plan for revenge. I'll get to Sauer another way if need be. No, this one will stop the tunnel project in its tracks."

Dread filled her, stomach muscles clenching in response. "Please don't ask me to kill George."

"You've wielded a weapon before. Why are you hesitant to do so now?"

"Self-defense is one thing, but...."

"Don't get your feathers ruffled, my canary." He squeezed her hand gently, and she marveled at how he'd reached out to her, not the other way around. He'd acted more demanding earlier when their sexual encounter started. "I won't force you or ask you to do anything that may make you uncomfortable. Sit back down. Where's the water?"

Leaning back into the chair, fully clothed once more, she pointed to another pitcher and glass she'd set at the opposite end of the room. A covered plate sat on the same table, and Luther groaned his appreciation at the sausage and bread slices. "Thank you for bringing me something to eat."

"What's the plan?"

He moved to the table, poured some water into the glass, and winked at her. "I'm going to blow up the machines, the tunnel entrance, and the railroad tracks." Pausing, he took a long swallow and then continued anew. "The entire camp will explode."

While he started to eat, she mulled over his words. A dozen questions flitted through her mind, along with the possibility he'd lost it being locked up in a closet for days. Sure, the fool had proved himself capable of great things a half dozen times if she believed the rumors. Rescuing scientists and others the Germans attempted to silence. Raiding soldier encampments and food stores, only to have the goods get in the hands of those who starved. The German government took the situations and flipped them into humanitarian efforts, all the while putting out a bounty on The Cursed ship and for the identity of their leader. They found out fast how Bolga lost control, but no one seemed to have a clue as to the identity of the top person. Evidenced by Luther's arrest and Sauer never giving him a second glance.

She considered the situation. "This idea, blowing up the camp. There'd need to be a whole train full of dynamite coming in to make this dream a reality."

"Not quite. I rode in with a couple of train cars of dynamite. Each week, a train comes with more to be used to help make the tunnel, where needed. I've got some experimental stuff coming, which will cause the dynamite to burn hotter if properly placed. We can get the whole thing to collapse. Setting the drillers at the right spot will have them melting in front of the tunnel's entrance and causing more problems. Then we rig a few additional bombs at different intervals along the train tracks, and supplies won't be received for months. Time the attack with a well-planned prison break, and there will be enough mayhem to cover our escape."

The idea could work. "But what experimental compound?"

"The material's called several names. RDX is one of them, another is hexagon."

She'd heard of hexagon before, thanks to an engineer who'd been begging the German government to let him try it out. "Yes, but how will you get the stuff? The German scientist who developed the formula didn't want to part with the recipe."

"I heard rumors he doesn't sympathize with the kaiser or the latest laws, so I reached out to him. We've worked out an agreement." He swallowed the last bite of sausage and bread, washing it down with the rest of the water. "I got everything rather cheap. All I had to do was volunteer to get his daughter out of the country. We'll pick her up after we complete the job."

A small twinge of jealousy unfurled in her chest at the idea of him playing rescue to another woman. "A beauty, no doubt."

He shook his head. "I don't care about her beauty, *dea.*"

The gleam in his eye and a slowly emerging smirk made him appear much like a predator on the grasp of catching his prey. Equally arousing and intimidating.

"Of course you care. When have you ever turned away a beautiful woman?"

"Far too often." He reached for her then, pulling her up out of the chair and wrapping his arms around her. "I've found myself always wanting someone else. A particular woman, with black hair, tawny skin, and gold flecks in her chocolate-brown eyes."

"I neither seek flattery nor want soppy platitudes."

"I'm truth telling. Something I'm starting to find more appealing. Will you help us with the plan?"

"Are you going to kill Sauer?" She'd never admit to relishing Luther's strength, nor the warmth and security he gifted her with when he held her.

"If I get the chance, I will, a non-negotiable for me. He needs to die."

Eva agreed with his deep-seated desire for revenge. She could relate better to it now and believe he'd find a way.

She wanted him dead, too, for Arik and her people, like Henri, now caught up in the German mess. The general was the one who'd caused the entire thing. He'd spearheaded the Nuremberg laws and sent Luther down his road with The Cursed and into her life. Except, she couldn't regret their meeting. No, she'd never trade those days they'd spent together. Even if they ended with her abandoned in Europe, she'd cherish this moment with him.

"In fact"—he stroked a path from the top of her forehead down her cheek, until his fingers rested under her chin—"I'll kill your fop-headed engineer, too. He dared to call you a *mulatto*."

George didn't know the term offended her. "I can't let you hurt him. He's no harm to anyone but himself. A bit foolish in his word choices, but he doesn't mean anything by it."

"What I'd give to have you defend me as much as you defend him. Since I've arrived, has he touched you?" A silly question, but she'd not hide the answer from him. Not when he pressed kisses to her neck, cheeks, and eyes, before pulling back and waiting for her reply.

"No." She shook her head. "I've taken to sleeping in a separate bedroom, claiming all manner of excuses, but, if not for his interest, Sauer would've killed me or sent me to this very work camp. I owe him for saving me from a worse fate."

Luther kissed her and enveloped her in a passionate embrace, all her soft spots matching to his hard ones. How quickly a discussion between the two of them, even an argument, could morph into something wonderful, like a butterfly emerging from a cocoon. Their tongues met in a dance, though the urgency found in their first joining stayed locked up. This meeting served the purpose of a renewed greeting and a promise for more.

They finally broke apart, panting. "Fine. For you, and for his keeping you safe, I'll let him live. But if he touches or insults you again, I'll kill him."

\*\*\*

Eva spent the next day going about her regular business. She waved George off to work from the front porch, readied a report for Sauer, and practiced a few staid, less combative tunes. Preparing for the requested concert was the best way to throw off the scent and make it appear she'd been properly chastised.

The worst part: not seeing Luther. He'd wound her up so tight, teased her to a state of discomfort after their conversation then not been able to provide release because Hans and Henri needed to put him back in his would-be cell. The frustration had continued into the night, made worse by George pressuring her to return to his bed. She complained of needing more rest due to nightmares, and he'd accepted her excuse. Luther would never know if she joined the engineer, but she would. She didn't want George touching her. No, she craved an outlaw's embrace, the passion of a devil of the first order.

A knock on the piano room door.

"Come in."

A soldier entered and bowed at the waist. "Frau, a Herr Reinhardt has arrived here to see you."

"Send him in," she replied with a wave of her hand. The name didn't sound familiar, but she imagined this might have something to do with the plans she and Luther had discussed the day before.

The soldier stepped backward and to the left, making way for a man of stocky build but less height. He stood a foot or so taller and his face was scarred horribly on the left side. If she'd seen only a profile, she'd have judged him some type of monster. The gypsy traveler, so noted by his boots and sash adorned with coins and bright colors, shut the door, leaving the soldier in the hallway. He greeted her with a wide smile, "Frau Sonne, so wonderful to meet you in person."

"I'm afraid I can't share the same sentiment as I have no clue who you are." She found his familiarity unsettling.

"I played at club Le Roux, many years ago, before the burns. You'd just arrived and sung a song so sweet. A gift beyond compare your voice. May I sit? My leg has gone stiff from the journey up the hill."

She nodded, the memory of this man before the burns, his face whole, surfacing. "You played the guitar? Had a very singular sound."

"You do remember."

"You didn't have the same features."

He chuckled. "The rumors you don't mince words or play to niceties are correct, then. No, I'd not been disfigured as I am now. At the time, I had a wife and a small son. The Germans killed them in a fire destroying nearly half of our encampment. Following the attack, they directed us to wander no more. Now, we are traders, not wanderers, and by consistently selling and transporting goods, we avoid persecution, until another reason for offense can be found."

"They kill or maim everything and everyone it seems." She rose from the piano bench, moving to the opposite door and pulling on the rope nearby to signal the kitchen for tea. "What brings you here?"

"My caravan travels through the area on its way to Calais and other northern ports. We bring vegetables and goods from the South of France for trade. We merely seek permission to stop here to trade with some of the soldiers, to provide entertainment for those weary, and, by week's end, we'll move on." The last sentence came with a wink.

There were more determinations to be made before she'd agree. "Do you carry any items for a particular person?"

"We've transported specific items for certain individuals in the past, and there may be such items in my possession."

The tea came then, brought by two female servants. One held the service, and another a tray of pastries, including some of the delicious apple strudel she'd been enjoying at every meal. They set things down, glancing at her companion with wary eyes. When he moved, one of the women jumped back, as if he'd contaminate her through contact.

Eva hissed her disapproval and dismissed them. "Let me apologize for their actions."

"No harm here. Females find me quite the beast as of late, and I don't blame them."

She poured the drinks, afternoon tea in a civilized piano room with a mixed-race female and a gypsy. Sauer would've remarked on the incident with disdain, no doubt. "How many are in your party?"

"We're a group of ten. Six females and four men. The men serve as protection. The females are free to interact with whomever they choose. None are married, and they are always in need of attention. They would provide excellent distractions along with some musical performances."

Eva took up her position back on the bench, teacup in hand. "Really? And you would like me to agree to these distractions?"

"It would make our travel easier and the job more exciting. Of course, your agreement might gain us favor." He sipped the tea, and she did the same. There were a lot of things not said. He'd all but openly admitted to being the one transporting Luther's explosive.

"I could speak to Herr Buckner about your staying here, but what of our soldiers or prisoners? They may find your presence too distracting."

"My hope is our presence will prove to alleviate their sorrows and suffering." The man weaved flowery sentences yet revealed no secrets. A talent she found herself unable to emulate. "We need two days, and you'll see a change in them, a release bound to make them happier."

George strolled in then, dusty and dirty. "Oh, I see you're entertaining Eva, my dove. Who's the fellow?" He stopped right inside the entrance to the room, on guard and uneasy.

"Let me introduce Herr—"

"Django Reinhold. The guide for a caravan of traders and a musician." The scarred man stood from his chair and approached the engineer, hand outstretched.

After a moment, George brushed his hands on his slacks in a futile attempt to clean them before embracing the handshake. "Ah, a musician. Does music bring you to our part of France? You're familiar with my Eva's talents?"

Django glanced between the two of them and then brightened. "Yes, I'm an admirer of her singing, to be sure. We seek rest for a few days and offer trade to the soldiers as well as a chance to pair my skills with Frau Sonne's, if she'll allow me the pleasure."

"Do you mean a concert?" Bless the fool's heart, George owned no worry or care in the world and spoke with such naivety. Eva couldn't have played it better. "The general mentioned he'd like Eva to do such a thing. Do you truly have the talent to keep up with her?"

"I'll certainly endeavor to try." The gypsy gave her the side-eye, her cue to jump in, and she did with gusto.

"Oh, I've no doubt I can whip him into shape by week's end, if we practice here or even at the caravan.

Please say yes, George. It will be a little concert to bring lots of happiness and energy to the men. They need it now more than ever." She clung to the engineer's arm, feigning adoration. *Damn.* Luther's touch had ruined her once again, and she'd be a liar if she tried to deny longing for more of his touches. Any way she could get them.

George pressed a kiss to her forehead, and she did her best to hide her disgust. "Dearest, if you're enthused about something after all the craziness of the past week, then, by all means, hold your concert. But no late night practices in this house. An engineer needs his sleep, after all."

"Any late practices will take place at the camp."

The Brit hunched his eyebrows and frowned. "I'm not sure it will be safe. After the evil anarchist and his band of cutthroats threatened you and me to my face, I don't want to take risks."

"Herr Buckner, I'll escort her with one of my guards if it makes you feel better. She'll be guarded as well as any of our merchandise." With his face all serious, for a second, she truly believed Django regarded her as property and not a person.

When George nodded, she wanted to stomp her foot. "All right," he agreed. "It's a plan. I'm for a bath, and I look forward to a spectacular concert on Saturday." He left the room, and the gypsy winked at her.

"He's not a very complex man, is he?"

She growled. "No, he isn't, and I'm not an object to be hauled around."

"Never said you were." Django picked up her hand and pressed a kiss to the back of it. "In fact, I said those words for his benefit alone. We can begin practice tomorrow."

Before she could respond or denounce his familiarity, he leaned in and whispered, "Who do I talk to, to find Luther?"

\*\*\*

Two taps on the cell door. The signal Hans stood on the other side. When the closet door creaked open, a laugh echoed within the small space. *Who the hell?*

"I never expected I'd see the day when you'd be brought so low." The accent and the jingle accompanying the steps gave his guest away.

"Django."

"The one and only." He turned and faced Hans. "Shut the door. Knock twice when dinner arrives."

His comrade did as requested, and Luther sat up from his prone position on the floor. Dietrich rested, propped up against the wall, silent, yet completely aware of the actions of the room. They'd practiced maneuvers in the dark, learning to operate bound. The chains and shackles had proved useful in keeping them in shape. As the last few days had passed, they'd become quite adept at moving quickly.

"Dinner? Have you come to cook for me?"

"No, but your sister's chef has. Sorella sent the girl and the first mate, Bastille, along with us after she intercepted a communiqué mentioning captured dissidents at this camp. Your sister figured you might be in trouble, and her instincts appear right. You're lucky you have such an intelligent ally on your side."

Luck didn't mean anything, but having the right people on your side did. So far, he'd employed and negotiated with the right people. "What's for dinner?"

"Cabbage soup. The chef knows a few things about digestion, and we have to prepare you for death."

Did he even want more details? Luther squatted back down and then sat on the floor, putting his legs out in front of him.

Django removed two cigarillos from his pocket. "These aren't your big cigars, but they will do in a pinch. How about you tell me how you got in here, and I'll share my latest."

Match light illuminated the room briefly as Django lit both cigarillos. The red tips bobbed in the dark after the match extinguished, and he somewhat made out his visitor's shadow as the red points got closer to him. The gypsy took a seat beside him and extended the wrapped tobacco. Luther clutched the end between two fingers and brought the treat to his lips for a drag. His body relaxed at the sweet scent of cherries filling the air

"I'm in here because of a woman scorned."

The gypsy laughed. "Really? What woman?"

"Eva." Her name came out soft and with an exhale of smoke, the A rolling off his lips. "Can't say I'm one of her favorite people, and the general bribed her. But he's pulled back from his agreement, and the death of our comrade swayed her to our side. Don't doubt for a second you can trust her."

"I don't trust any woman, ever. But I'll honor your word unless she proves otherwise."

Luther let out another tunnel of smoke. "If she proves otherwise, I'll take care of her myself." The idea of anyone touching her swamped him with anger and frustration. The suggestion she'd go back on their agreement, after they'd sealed it with kisses, intimacy, flooded his body with anger. He'd turned on someone with less connection, but their bond—

"Fine. Whatever. I've got some ideas to play with yours. Eva's agreed to host a concert with me this weekend. We'll perform for the soldiers, act the distraction. By then, you and your man here will be free and able to rig up the explosives I brought with the dynamite and the drills." The excitement in Django's voice surprised him. He'd been doubtful when they first talked.

"What's changed? You didn't exactly believe in my idea before." Another puff and the cigarillo appeared half gone. *Sad.*

"I received a demonstration courtesy of your sister. Let's say we ran into a bit of trouble with an inspection, and, instead of turning over the cargo, we used a bit of it. She certainly doesn't pull punches, and her husband is crafty, too."

Luther remembered his brother-in-law and still sported a scar where the fool had knocked him out with an electo wand nearly a year prior. If not for his love of Sorella, Luther would've killed the man faster than a coil gun reload. "Yes, they are both quite capable. Now, how are we getting out of here?"

"You'll have to die."

\*\*\*

He'd scarfed down three bowls of cabbage soup.
The stuff tasted awful, but, according to the plan, it'd
pay off to drink the horrible meal. They'd had three
days of nothing but cabbage soup with fish, and now
the time drew near. Dietrich had said prayers and
expressed doubt in the plan, but Luther would trust his
sister. She wouldn't kill him, not yet. At least, he hoped
not. Technically, with her supplying the explosives,
she'd already fulfilled her debt to him.

And he'd always believed if his sister wanted
someone dead, she'd do it herself, not send a chef to
take care of the job.

Two loud bangs of a fist against the door, and in
came two men and a woman holding a lantern. One of
the men was Hans, the other he recognized as his
sister's right hand, Bastille. How the hell the Germans
weren't tormenting him, he didn't know. The big
Frenchman with skin as dark as soil wore no uniform,
but gypsy clothing.

"What's he doing here? He'll expose us all."

148

Hans shrugged his shoulders. "He wouldn't allow the woman to leave his sight. Something about a promise. Don't worry. We avoided detection. Django and a few of the others started a big card game, and everyone's watching."

"Fine. Shut the door."

Once the door was secured, with Hans standing outside once more as a sentry, the woman approached, wearing a billowing blouse and skirts, her head covered in a scarf, her figure anonymous thanks to her disguise. "I'm Bonita. Do you remember me?"

She held up the lantern, her skin appearing lighter than his own, with a few red tendrils poking out of the multi-colored head scarf. Eyes of blue, swirled with green, met his. *Buon Dio*. He recalled this woman. She was the same age as him, pressed into service for his sister. Another trained to serve, but as a lady's maid and companion. She would've taken the blame or fall for any mistakes and acted as a cover for his sister once placed on assignment. "*Si*, you stayed with her this long?"

"*Naturalemente*. Why would I leave? Unless at her insistence."

"Why did she send you?"

She held up a small bottle. "Because I'm the only one who can smell this scent and administer the correct dosage. Have you eaten all the soup sent for you both?"

Luther waited for Dietrich to nod, and then he acknowledged her as well. "How long will this take?"

"I hope for an immediate effect, but it may be a few hours. You will feel pain, but without it the process does not sound as real. As far as anyone will be able to tell, you've died of ruptured organs."

Dietrich crossed himself. Luther laughed at the idea. Death never scared him. No, he found himself more scared of becoming overly attached to certain people than of death. "How can you be sure?"

"When no wounds are present, no weapons, no bruising, people naturally reach such a conclusion. Besides, German-employed doctors won't waste time on prisoners. Your deaths mean nothing." She spoke truth. Their deaths would go uninvestigated.

Dietrich became uneasy when she approached him first. "Poison. You mean to poison us. I don't trust it. How can you be sure we'll wake?"

"I can't be. In fact, there are no guarantees, except freedom, either from this prison or this world."

Either one worked for Luther. He moved to his knees and locked eyes with his man. "I'll hold you down, or you'll suck it up. This is the only way we're getting out of here, by fake death or a real one. Let it be on our terms, not theirs."

Dietrich took a few deep breaths then nodded. Bonita moved closer. "Tilt your head back and open your mouth."

She twisted open a glass bottle, removed a dropper, and squeezed the top. Five, no, six droplets of clear liquid fell into his mouth. Dietrich's face said it all, his mouth contorting in disgust. Then she turned to Luther. "Have you made peace?"

"I'm very familiar with torment. Get on with it."

"Very well."

The dropper hovered over his open mouth, and, for a split second, he reflected on how he might never see Eva again. Then the first drop hit.

# Chapter Nine

Eva stood on her terrace, puffing on a cigarillo and searching for the stars. In the distance, music played, and voices echoed up from the campsite. The same as they had every night this week. Now, on the eve of their performance, she'd been blown off by Django for a card game. One far too dangerous for her to attend, what with men being there. She flicked her ash into the air. *Damn men.* George had sided with the gypsy, too. He'd gone down to catch a couple of rounds, interested in testing his skill.

"Not often can a man get in on a game," were his words of justification.

Meanwhile, she remained alone, and Django encouraged her to rest her voice after practicing hard all week. They'd worked on several songs, some new to her, and others new to him. A mixture of acceptable jazz tunes, German folk, French tunes, and one musical number from a new musical popular in America. Between vigorous rehearsals, she'd shared her familiarity with the camp, the latest news from George on their supplies and machinery.

The gypsy had worked with his fellows to make maps and appointed Henri to transport the information to Luther's man. She'd wanted to meet with him again, to feel Luther's lips one last time before everything went crazy. No matter how many times she asked, Django would never say how he planned to get Luther and the other man out of captivity. Based on the discussions, they'd needed Eva and Henri to make everything work.

She stamped out her smoke in the little tin tray by her feet. They considered themselves smart for leaving her out of the loop, verbally described as splitting information. A stupid idea and she'd told the gypsy the very same during practice the previous evening. He'd sparred back at her if she hadn't turned Luther over in the first place, they wouldn't be in this situation.

"What the hell does a gypsy know?"

Then George's Jeep pulled up, jarring her from her angry musings. She ran downstairs and reached the bottom step as the parlor room door slammed against the wall.

"Dearest, what's wrong? Did you lose?" Her questions went unanswered as George poured a full glass of brandy and swallowed its entire contents.

"Ah, much better," he said, wiping at his mouth with a coat sleeve.

"Tell me what happened?"

"They are dead." He reached for the decanter and poured himself another. The man didn't usually drink so liberally.

"Who?"

"The men Sauer captured. Both of them, twisted and contorted, with pained expressions, lying on the floor of the closet."

Her gut clenched, and she stuffed her hand into her mouth, biting hard to prevent any sound from emerging. The possibility seemed unreal. They were supposed to escape, not die. She moved her fingers aside to mumble, "How?"

"Doctor says some sort of hemorrhaging. The soldiers guarding them have been instructed to throw the bodies in the sea in case there's a virus or infection." George gulped down a second glass.

Eva's stomach lurched at the idea of being stuck in the camp without Luther, without a chance for escape. Now, she couldn't risk anything. The idiot mercenary actually made her believe they'd succeed. Even the damn gypsy convinced her, but they'd been hoping for a miracle it seemed. No, she'd been hoping. She'd have to play out her days here. Use George as a means to help her people somehow, get closer to the foolish man and barter sex to control him.

"Come here, gorgeous. Hold me." Her would-be lover extended his arms, and she went to him. No choice really.

He pulled her in close. "I've missed you in our bed. Tell me you'll give up sleeping in the other room and come back to me."

The idea of being with him so soon after Luther's death did the opposite of providing comfort. No, she wanted to swaddle herself in the memories of their last time together, even go to the spot where they'd joined. Stupid, sentimental emotions awakened by his touch, and he'd gone and died before they even explored the possibilities. Another reminder of how a woman couldn't depend on a man. Even so, her heart ached. "I can't. What you said bothers me greatly. I'm not comfortable with death."

"You're too fragile. I understand. But think it over and let me have a chance to heal you."

*Oh*! She'd love to kill him, though. For a brief second, she'd wished she let Luther get rid of him. He truly believed his brand of ridiculous, too. Before she pulled away from his embrace, she made sure to clear her face of emotion, to keep things neutral, but let her eyes droop, as if exhausted. "I'll think it through. One more night without exertion?"

"To bed with you. You've worked so hard practicing all week. Django told me. An interesting character, this gypsy. Quite brutal in appearance, too."

"He's hideous. Good night." She didn't wait for him to respond before walking to the back of the house and out the servants' entrance in the kitchen. Keeping to the shadows, she skirted the building. The soldiers on guard duty were telling each other jokes and smoking and none remarked on her passage. She made it to a copse of trees on the other side of the road. After a few minutes of bobbing and weaving to keep her trail uneven, she came to Django's camp on the hilltop.

She went straight to his wagon and banged on the door.

He hollered, "One minute."

When he finally opened it up, he stood there, chest and arms exposed. Extensive burns ran down the entire left side of his body and his left arm. "Frau Sonne? Usually, a lady knocking on a man's door this late at night means one thing only."

She pushed him aside and climbed the steps into the place he called home.

"All right. If you need me in that capacity, I'm yours," he replied before shutting the door.

Before he could say another world, she whirled to face. "Are they really dead?"

"Who?"

"Luther and his man. George came to the house and said their guards found them dead. The guards are friends of theirs. So?" She wrung her hands as if trying to drain the blood out of her skin. She'd been lied to so many times.

"If they say so, then the pair must be."

A roar in her ears, a rush of rage, and she officially lost it. A knife lay on top of a box beside her. A knife she grabbed and then, with quick finesse, maneuvered the tip against Django's throat. He tried to dodge the encounter, but she was ready. So ready. Years of defensive lessons from Janken's friends came back. She pivoted to the right and swept his legs out from under him. Once he was prone, she stepped on his wrist, cutting off his attempt to reach for an electo wand by the door.

He moaned, and she moved in, sitting on top of his chest, knees burrowing into pressure points near his armpits and the knife right where she wanted it, near the major neck artery. "I can fake the niceties, but only for so long, and I'm tired of being bullied. Tired of the lies I keep being told because people believe lying to be in my best interest. So, you get one more chance, and if I don't believe you, then the plan ends. I don't care anymore."

"He's alive."

Funny how she didn't have to ask twice after physically threatening his life. "Where is he?"

"Being dumped on the ground outside camp. Hans and Henri will stay with them until they awake then come back in time to get everything in place for the performance. As soon as we give the signal, they will trigger the detonators." He fell silent, and she stared into those dark eyes. They appeared shifty, normally, but his face had lost any sign of amusement as soon as she'd assumed a hunter's position.

"He still wants to carry through with the plan?"

"Yes. Do I pass the canary's test for release?"

She eased off him, trailing the knife away from his neck, but still close to the skin as she came to a standing position.

"He never said you were capable of such things."

"When I'm pushed too far, you'd be surprised what I'm capable of." The threat made, she threw the door to the wagon open and fled back to the house.

She'd be damn sure she was ready.

\*\*\*

They'd waited all day, munching dry biscuits and sipping on the water bottles Henri and Hans brought them from the camp. Luther went over the plans, drilled them into their heads. Hans would assume the position as a prison guard the reasoning being the dissidents' demise put him back on regular duty. Dietrich, Henri, and he would line up the drillers, set the explosives, and run the wiring. They'd split up and move between the communications tent, the train, and the concert hall.

Everything revolved around timing. A small cart hauled by a donkey showed up in the late afternoon, driven by Bastille. The dark-skinned man provided two additional uniforms so Luther and Dietrich could finalize their disguise.

He provided belts and weapons as well. "They will begin the concert at sundown, in approximately two hours. They called dinner early and had already herded the workers to their tents and locked them in."

"Good. Do we ride with you, then?"

Bastille shook his head. "No, there's no place to hide you. Also, Django wanted me to tell you Sauer arrived on the afternoon train. The locomotive has three cars filled with prisoners. They plan to unload them, but not until tomorrow."

"Shit!" The least offensive of the expletives bouncing around in his brain. He threw the water bottle to the ground then regained his composure. After running both hands through his hair and slicking it back, he then put the cap Bastille gave him in place. "We'll play it by ear. We blow the tracks then disconnect the cars quarter of a mile away, blowing the locks on the doors."

"Sir," Henri spoke up, "can't we take them with us? They might be hunted down."

"My job involves getting our group and Django's out of here fast and speedy. We can't risk being weighed down by people who are going to die anyway."

Henri's mouth dropped open. "But, those people—"

"Are not our problem," Hans finished for him.

They packed up then, and the men began the trek back to camp, while Bastille rode off in his cart. The trek proved easy enough, and the others sang songs, nursery rhymes, and other tunes they'd known since childhood. Luther recognized a few but used the walk to contemplate Henri's reaction. Would Eva feel the same way about those caught on the train? Yet, transporting them would bring unwanted attention. His sister would find a way to save them. She'd become the avenging angel of the downtrodden. He still relied on the old, safe ways. Cut out those not needed, so his crew survived.

By the time they reached the edge of the camp, coming up on the guard shack next to the train, he'd made his decision. Before he got a chance to voice the changes, though, Dietrich signaled they'd been seen.

A soldier called out to them. Hans took point and listened to the man prattle on about a late night of whoring and drinking in a farmhouse to the west. The soldier laughed, while another inside the shack picked up a headset.

Luther motioned to Henri and Diet to move to the side, and he pressed the small button on the EMP bomb. Besides uniforms, Bastille had given them plenty of toys. After a kiss to the metal ball, he rolled it at the shack. The ball hit the foot of one soldier, the small, muted explosion knocking him to the ground. Hans moved in and snapped the talking soldier's neck, while Dietrich charged for the small building, ran inside, and disabled the soldier there.

He needed more men. Bastille would've been great, but the first mate claimed his allegiances belonged with a particular cook, and he'd sworn to Sorella he'd protect the woman at all costs. The one thing Luther wanted to avoid was crossing his sister. So, they'd have to sacrifice someone else for the job.

"Henri, you'll stay in the shack. We can't have anyone re-taking this ground."

They heaped the dead soldiers' bodies into the far corner of the room. The young man didn't seem very confident in staying there. "I'm not sure—"

"Playing sentry is a great idea. You will also monitor communications. We won't be in contact until we get back here, but if anyone messages out to see how things are, you can reassure them."

"What do I say?" Henri sat at the communication station, coil rifle in his lap.

"Tell them the other guard has gone out to survey the train, and you're on post. They will believe you, and, in two hours, we'll be long gone."

The boy nodded, and the group left, moving swift and silent through the camp. Hans darted off toward the prisoners' tents while Luther and Dietrich headed toward the tunnel and the drillers stored right inside the entrance. The strum of a guitar and a lilting voice filtered down from the hill toward the back.

Dietrich lit an entrance lantern, and light refracted off at least five drilling machines. Crates of dynamite were stored at the entrance, along with a container with a raven etched into the top especially for him. Things would be exploding tonight.

*\*\**

Eva had never felt less enthused about singing but kept belting out the words to a gypsy folk tune with as much gusto as she could muster. No sense in apologizing for her behavior toward Django the previous night. They'd continued like nothing happened. He'd displayed the same amount of kindness toward her, but the other gypsies stayed away.

Now, they all gathered their belongings. Django delivered the instructions himself. As soon as the music started, the gypsies would dismantle the camp, with the exception of the stage constructed out of one of the wagons.

A simple but down-home design, with its curtains made from heavy woolen blankets, gave an authenticity to the country type music they'd agreed to play. Sauer had shown up, courtesy of the noon train. He'd received the communication about the concert and claimed he didn't want to miss the "hedonistic display." Coming and going at will was one of the privileges of being a German. *Ha.* Everyone else got put on the kidnapping and imprison lists by virtue of looks and genealogy. She'd no doubt Sauer's spies had already relayed detailed information about the visiting traders. The general regarded them as unclean, of course.

The general sat near the front, on the edge of a row—all the better if he needed to escape. His bodyguards were stationed close to him. Yet, they'd all become relaxed as the songs went on. Between Eva's voice, Django's throaty sound, and the guitar strumming and picking, they received plenty of hoots and hollers from the audience.

Happy men were made jollier by a beverage concoction of the visiting cook. She'd shown up with a barrel before the show started and handed out glass after glass. They drank openly, without a care, which surprised her, but Sauer welcomed the efforts being afforded to keep the men in good spirits.

As she let the last notes of the song fade from her throat, the crowd burst into applause. Eva bowed, and when she glanced up, her eyes met Luther's. He stood at the back of the group, away from all the rows of chairs and makeshift stools assembled to accommodate everyone. Some still chose to stand, used to it after so long. But he'd found a way to meet her gaze between a sea of men.

Yes, she'd imagined him all day, not sure if Django told the truth or if tonight would mean she'd be dead. She tried to redirect his gaze toward Sauer, and he finally got the message. Her singing partner strummed the intro chords to their final number, "Donkey Serenade." The musical bit served as the signal.

She adjusted her blouse and glanced down at her boot tops. She'd stuck to a muted green, not too unlike the soldier's uniforms. She'd enjoyed pairing the standard-issue slacks with a matching, long-sleeved blouse. Ready to make a break for it, she took a deep breath then a slow exhale as another gypsy joined them onstage playing a piccolo. The high notes were her cue to begin.

The lyrics were silly and quite humorous, and she played things up by meeting George's eyes several times. He returned her attentions and even gave her a wink as encouragement. No doubt he'd be sad when she left, but he'd survive. Nor did she believe he'd be heartbroken.

Her performance required prancing around the stage and pretending Django was a donkey. She even placed a pair of brown fabric ears held together with wire on his head. The crowd laughed and put their index fingers on top of their heads, demonstrating the ears. They called out to her that she should sing to them, the donkey soldiers.

The instrumental intro gave her a chance to seek out Luther again, but she didn't see him. No, instead she got a glimpse of the disgust on Sauer's face. She blew a kiss in his direction, which George pretended to snap from the air for himself. *Bless him.*

When the last few bars hit, the ground shook beneath the stage. She fell to one knee and made damn sure her mouth opened in shock. Django stopped playing, and then an explosive blasted a short distance away, followed by  four successive discharges seconds apart. Soldiers went scrambling down the hill toward the camp, right as the communications building erupted. Wood flew through the air and fire lit up the sky.

She dared a glimpse at her singing partner. He'd already flipped his guitar to his back and moved toward her. After he helped her to a standing position, they sprinted toward the stage steps. Hell had officially broken loose.

# Chapter Ten

Luther had already started moving toward the stage before the bombs went off. He needed to get within range of Sauer if he ever wanted to give the general his new look. But he'd failed to take into consideration the number of soldiers separating him from his prey, and they'd all come running to the exit once the first bomb exploded.

When the concussions began to rattle the ground, a huge herd of soldiers moved toward him. He feinted to the right, avoiding the majority of them, but Sauer's bodyguards converged to protect their leader.

Django and Eva dashed for the stairs to get off the stage. She hadn't melted under pressure—his girl never did.

Someone ran into him, and he shoved them back into the crowd swarming to follow orders, most likely the engineer's. George climbed up onto the stage and shouted in German for the men to get water tanks and to use sandbags to put out any fires. They'd soon figure out the explosives used would have to burn out on their own, and a little water or sand wouldn't stop them, especially with hot metal added to the mix. There'd be a great disaster cleanup ahead.

Sauer shouted at Eva and Django to stop. His bodyguards moved to intercept them, but Django drew an electo wand. The blue from the electricity being activated was easily visible as the gypsy engaged the guards. Luther surged forward, knocking people out of his way. He'd get to the bodyguards first then take out the general.

Eva refused to cower, standing tall and grabbing her microphone. Luther stood only a few feet away, and then two soldiers rushed at him, grabbing him by the shoulders and trying to convince him to go and help them. Unbuckling his knife, he slashed at the first one, sticking the young man in the belly. The second one pulled his blade, and the battle ensued.

Flipping the knife, Luther put the blade against his forearm, while he circled his opponent. The blond soldier lunged first and slashed at his arm. Dodging to the left, Luther leaned in and nicked his ribs. While his opponent groaned, Luther went for the kill, crouching down to sweep the man's legs out from under him. He shoved his knees into the youth's chest, and sliced his throat.

He'd never found mercy for those attempting to prevent him from reaching his goal. Standing back up, he twirled around scanning for Eva. She held a chair high, ready to crash it down on the bodyguard not engaged with Django. The impact brought the guard to his knees, and then the sound of a single gunshot rang out.

Eva stumbled. Red pooled above her waist, staining her blouse. He howled, something loud and furious. Charging forward, he reached the guard still engaged with Django and shoved a knife into his back. He ripped the blade out, and blood gushed from the wound as the man fell. The gypsy powered down his wand and rushed to Eva's side.

Luther ended the other bodyguard then shoved Django out of the way. "Get the wagon ready."

The gypsy nodded, struggled to a standing position, and moved away.

Eva coughed. "I'm so happy to see you again."

"Don't talk, little canary. Save your words and your strength. I'm getting you out of here." Luther glanced behind him. Sauer was already gone. *Damn.* In the end, the asshole didn't matter, Eva living did. They'd need a doctor and a safe place. They had to reach the train.

He started to move toward the side of the tent, determined to rip a damn hole through the canvas to get through if the gypsy didn't do it first. Then the Brit's shaky voice sounded behind him. "Put her down, now."

Refusing to acknowledge the fool and remembering his promise to Eva not to kill him, Luther kept moving. The tent side ripped open, and Hans stood on the other side. "Wagon's waiting, Captain. Our chance to catch the train will be lost if we don't hurry."

His man climbed into the back of the wooden box first and took his lover's body with ease, but not for long. As soon as Luther managed to get in the box, he grunted at Hans to hand her over. No one would touch her again except for him and a doctor.

She reached up and touched his face. "Your hair is growing back."

"Want me to shave it?"

Another cough and a shake of her head. "No. I like you all wild and crazy. Though I doubt I'll get to see your hair grown out again."

Those words could be left unspoken. The idea she wouldn't survive until they got on the train or even after clawed at his heart like little knives raking across the surface. She'd given so much for others, for him, and he'd repaid her by putting her life at risk again and again.

"You will if I have anything to say about it. I'm going to make this up to you, *dea.*" He motioned for the blanket next to Hans, and his comrade tossed it to him. Covering her body, he used it to renew the pressure on the wound and to keep her warm. "We're almost to the train. Hold on."

When they finally cleared the edge of the camp, they could see several cars loaded with gypsies and workers. Bodies of dead soldiers littered the ground. He focused on Eva, putting Hans in charge of making sure the train got started with no whistle and no warning to anyone they would depart.

Django helped them settle in one of the cars, laying blankets out into a pallet for Eva. The gypsy musician even found a doctor. More aptly, a witch doctor, for the woman demanded water and opened a box of herbs, liquid concoctions, smelling salts, and random metal instruments. He wanted to demand the woman stop her conjuring, but Eva's clammy skin and loss of blood arrested him. Before long, his men called for his shooting capabilities on the roof. It seemed soldiers in Jeeps pursued them. So Luther left Eva to the care of the witch-woman and another gypsy who vowed she'd be safe in their hands. He pressed a kiss to his lover's sweaty hand, in case.

*If she doesn't live—* He growled and stalked to the boxcar door. With his anger properly channeled, he'd put down as many Germans as possible in vengeance and hunt Sauer to the end of the earth. The general wouldn't be able to avoid him now. Not after this.

\*\*\*

The sweet chirps of birds woke her, and she jerked up in bed, startled. The pain hit her hard, a strong twinge in her lower right side. "Damn," she cried.

"Gunshot wounds typically hurt for many months. Hold a moment." A gypsy woman approached and put a glass in Eva's hands, before fluffing the pillows behind her back. "Now lean back."

"Where I am?" The pain eased as Eva relaxed against the stacked pillows.

"Drink, then I tell you."

So she drank the mixture of water and something else. "What's in this?"

"Garlic and other herbs. They will help with the healing and protect against more fever."

Eva downed the rest of the water and handed the cup off. "Tell me now. Where am I?"

"You're in Reinhold's camp, Western France. Not far from the river." Those words barely meant anything. The woman's lack of clear communication didn't do her much good. A dozen rivers existed in the west, and the camp traveled, so no telling where they'd stopped for the day.

"How long have I been out?"

The woman shook her head. "I say no more and will get the giant. He tells you more." Then the gypsy left before she could ask additional questions. She waited, impatiently, taking in her surroundings. Bright red, blue, and green blankets covered her body. She wore a flannel nightgown with her legs left bare. Hopefully, the old woman had been tasked with removing her clothes.

She remembered the end of the concert, the explosion, attacking one of Sauer's bodyguards, and then the pain. Sliding her hand down her body, she made contact with her bare leg right above her hip. Inching the nightgown up, she touched thick dressings that lay underneath along her stomach.

The tent flap flew back, and in strolled Django. "You're awake. Thank heavens."

"You're a giant?"

He leaned on a cane and took up residence on a small wooden stool at the end of her bed. His humor at the question confined to a small chuckle. "Not me. Your mercenary captain. He's been a big bear ever since you got injured. Didn't want to leave your side, nor did he believe anyone beyond his own doctor capable of healing you. I'll need to make the doctor aware of your change."

Her heart clenched at his mention of Luther. She remembered him lifting her into his arms, holding a hand tight against her wound, and calling her *dea*. Then he'd left her on the train, swearing as he went. "Where's Luther?"

"Busy, at the moment. There are many plans to make and a lot of information to sort through. He's trying to find the general."

"Luther didn't kill him already?"

Django shook his head. "No, the man disappeared, and we ran out of time."

Nausea swamped her belly. "How long have I been out?"

"Three days."

"*Merde.*" She hated being useless or even sick, but sleeping for three days?

"*Non, madame.* You have no reason to be upset. The bullet was removed, but a fever persisted. When the good doctor suggested bleeding you, Luther kicked him out of the room. My grand-*mére* took care of you and *voila*! You're going to be fine."

An incorrect assessment. She'd be fine once she beheld Luther, once he told her about the camp and why Sauer got away and the million other questions she wanted answers to. She'd pepper her visitor with as many as he'd let her. "Who shot me? Where's Henri?"

Django stood and moved toward the tent opening. "Let's save the questions for after the doctor sees you. I'll let Luther know so he can visit, too."

The man who shot her didn't matter. She'd survived, and needed to get to her club. Once her wound healed, she'd be free or as free as one could be on a dictator-ruled continent. As much as she longed to launch out of bed, a wave of exhaustion grabbed her again. She snuggled back under the covers for a nap in the hope Luther would arrive soon.

\*\*\*

"She's asked for you." Django's voice rippled through his cabin.

"Eva's awake?" He pulled his gaze from the intelligence reports on his desk to the cigar-smoking gypsy in his doorway.

"Yes, and she wants to know who shot her, where Henri is, and where you are. At first, she kept the requests minimal, but she's starting to get annoying."

"Giving you too much trouble, eh?" Luther shoved his chair back and stood, glancing down at his clothes. He hadn't changed in a day and slept every night next to her bed, on a tiny godforsaken stool. She'd tossed and turned, mumbled, and even hummed a few bars here and there. But this morning, he'd been called away by the arrival of *Maledetto* and information on the general. A few of the reports had conflicting information, but they all conveyed the end result. The sniveling coward who liked to shoot women had holed up outside Paris.

"She's a handful."

"I'll clean up and then see her. Has she eaten dinner yet?"

Django shook his head in response. "Have you decided what you're going to do?"

He pressed a button on his desk, alerting Roscoe to start the preparations for the ship's departure. "There's only one thing to do." Luther removed his knife and sheath from his belt, along with the coil gun he'd been carrying since the train ride. He would take no chances, not unless he could heavily predict the outcome.

"What?"

Luther grinned wide. "I'm going to hunt the bastard Sauer down and get rid of our problem once and for all."

# Chapter Eleven

When he flipped the tent flap back, he'd expected to see her still flat on the bed, pale and barely conscious. He'd become familiar with the image of Eva in such a state, broken and hurt , over the last several days. Hearing she'd awakened failed to remove the image from his brain, but seeing her sitting up in bed with her eyes alert made him believe in miracles.

She smiled when she saw him, the fire pit in the center of the room not doing much by way of lighting, but it proved decent for keeping the room warm.

"Is there food for me?" She pointed at the tray in his hand.

He removed the lid. "The doc wanted me to bring down some soup. Nothing fancy, but there's some bread for dipping and—"

"Bring it over here. I'm famished." To hear those words, to see her face light up at the prospect of soup, acted as a salve over the open wound of the day. She always did that, provided light when none existed.

Walking over, he set the tray on her lap then dragged the stool from the end of the bed next to her.

The damn thing proved uncomfortable, but her pallet would break under his weight. She dug in right away, no preliminaries. Dipping chunks of bread into the broth, she slurped the result into her mouth.

"Tastes good?"

He barely heard her muffled, "Delicious."

"All right," he responded with a chuckle. "I'm sure the doctor already told you he removed the bullet. You should make a full recovery since the fever has broken, and you can get out of bed for short periods of time starting tomorrow, provided you don't try to stretch, bend, reach, or lift anything. It will mess with the stitches."

"Tell me something I haven't heard already." She grinned at him and shook her head as if he was silly for reviewing the same stuff over and over again. Better than the truth, a truth to send her happiness plummeting.

"Henri died."

The lump of bread in her hand splashed into the rest of the broth with a thunk. Soup sloshed out of the bowl and splattered against the tray. "How?"

"A stray bullet caught him as the train pulled out of the camp. He'd taken up position with me on the sentry spot on top of the car near the caboose. The

German bastard got lucky, but his luck ran out when I pinched him with my own bullet in the head."

Her hands flew up to her face, wiping at the tears starting to flow. "Where's the body?"

"We couldn't hold it, due to the length of the journey and his injuries. We buried him about twelve hours after we got here. Once you're up and moving, I'll take you over there."

She slapped her hands against the blankets, the force absorbed by the material. "He was a kid, a young man. Those damn recruiters promised him the chance to send home food and money. Liars, all of them. Why did he go up there instead of one of your guys?"

Those gray eyes stared him down, narrow and with a storm brewing inside. He hoped she didn't blame him; when the fault could be laid at her feet from the get-go. "One of my guys would've been there if we weren't down to three. The situation proved a little more difficult than my expectations."

They'd been shorthanded, with Dietrich manning the controls, Hans guarding at the front of the train, and still needed two people posted in the back. Their choices were limited to him and Henri since Bastille had disappeared with Bonita sometime during the madness

Her sobs were nearly silent, and the jarring movements of her shoulders heaving up and down couldn't be good for her stitches. Luther leaned in, moving the tray to the floor beside them, and pulled her close. "I'm sorry, *dea*. Those words—his death is not your fault. We all have to be responsible for our own decisions. Henri went out protecting people he cared about and trying to get them to safety."

"Yes, but you're right. If not for me…he'd still be here." She let out a fresh sob, and more tears spilled.

Luther rubbed her shoulders, then her back, all the while trying to change the topic. "Honey, you should feel sorry for what you did to me."

"You're not making me feel better, and you're an ass. Who shot me?"

He wouldn't apologize for his feelings, even if they minimized another's death, someone he never had a chance to acquaint himself with. There would be no hiding the truth from her, either. "Sauer did, right after you hit his goon with a chair. Your lover threatened me if I didn't put you down, and I ignored him."

"George? Threatened you?"

"Do you find such a thing impossible?" He leaned back to make eye contact. "For people to threaten me?"

"Surprising really."

He leaned in again to smell her hair, sap that he was—he'd been thinking for days on the matter of her twisting his insides, the uncontrollable rage at the idea she wouldn't survive. "Is it so surprising to believe you affect people? Affect me?"

"I tend to be a diversion for most." She always downplayed her effect.

"Really? A diversion? I slashed a man's throat trying to get to you. I wouldn't leave your side and about killed my doctor when he said he had no idea if you'd survive. You're more than a diversion."

She touched his cheek, and he wrapped his hand around hers. "What are you saying, Luther?"

"Years ago when we met...when I left, I believed you'd be safer than being with me. Safer in France where the cultural views appeared a little less strict. The Cursed, we always found ourselves in dangerous situations, and I couldn't protect you. What I'm trying to say is...I love you."

Eva jerked her hand out of his, and the movement made her hiss through her teeth at the sharp pain in her side. She kept forgetting she'd sustained an injury and sat useless and left to her lover's cruel mercies. "You're screwy. Messing with those explosives and experimental poisons messed you up something good."

"Don't pull away, not when I'm on the level here."

"Really? Bringing up the past again and then telling me you love me." She put her face in her hands. The possibility made her chest ache. Some wild yearning need to confess the same feelings for him rose, too. Those urges occurred from the moment she woke, working their way into a crescendo when she added in how she almost died, he'd saved her and refused to leave her behind. "You could have left me there."

"Never. Don't act a piker. You're too strong, too tough to run from me." He slid two fingers underneath her chin, lifting her head and then pressing his lips against hers. She stubbornly wanted to stay strong, to deny a response, but when he swiped his tongue across her lips, she gasped, and he found a way in. The pursuit was still far more gentle then before.

She loved the taste of him. The way he stoked the slow fire in her body, increasing the heat and making her want to shove the blankets away, to bare all. He'd kissed her like this when they met. They'd spent days wrapped in each other's arms, mapping their bodies with hands, tongues, and mouths. Skin to skin, nothing between them. The bandages around her abdomen prevented the same amount of contact, but she couldn't help craving more.

When he finally broke away, they were both panting. "Better slow down, *dea*. I don't want to get you in trouble with those stitches."

"What if I don't care?" She'd gone a bit screwy from his kiss.

"I'd call you a liar. Besides, you never responded to my confession."

"What confession?" He could say it a million times, and she still wouldn't believe him. "You left me before, what's different now, almost dying? I don't want to be the afterthought or the convenient option."

He stood from the stool and glowered at her. "I'll show you convenient."

Then he pulled all the covers back except for one, wrapping the blanket around her before lifting her into his arms. She didn't fight, afraid it would hurt the stitches. "Where are you taking me?"

"To my place." He marched out of the tent and toward the ship's platform, still in a lowered position since he came down. Several gypsies milled around a campfire, including Django, who eyed them. "Tell the doc, don't tell him. I don't care, gypsy."

Luther's words kept the musician in his place, and Eva laughed. "You're silly."

"If the goal gets you to believe me, then I'll be silly."

His words made her a bit breathless and shocked. "Believe what?"

"In my feelings for you."

The platform rose, lifting them into the sky, the air chilly around them. She leaned back and gazed up at the night sky, clear of clouds with a half-moon on the rise. Stars shown bright, a thousand of them.

"I believe you have feelings...for me."

He chuckled. "So confident in them, are you? You think I'm still playing games."

The metal-infused rope screeched to a halt as the platform locked in place. Men worked or relaxed around them. Sparks from a laser on an EMP net, laughter from a group making jokes and sipping drinks. An environment aboard the *Maledetto* she wasn't as familiar with. Her last visit everyone had been silent, serious, and...*okay.* "Yes, you're good at emotional games. Fool me once, shame on you. Fool me twice, shame on me."

He carried her into a corridor and on through different sections of the ship until they reached the end of the passage. A nudge with his boot heel and the door in front of them creaked open. Inside, a small Tesla lantern generated light in the room, but the primary source of illumination came from the moonlight streaming in the giant window. No, little portholes for him. The captain had glorious quarters.

Instead of giving her a view out the window, he took her to the right beyond some partition and deposited her on the bed, though more gently than she'd ever suspected. He inspected her for a minute, left her side, and came back with the lantern. "I'll check your stitches real quick."

"I'm fine."

He shushed her and pulled back the thin blanket. "So you've said before, and you've lied before."

A lot of meaning went into those words and accompanied a fresh reminder of her betrayal, the loss of Henri. How did one forgive themselves for something they regretted? He unknotted the sheet tied around her waist then pulled back the clean, white cotton cloth they'd piled up over the stitches. The area around the stitching proved moist and devoid of puffiness, yet they needed to keep everything dry. He trailed his finger above the line of string used to successfully close a hole torn in her flesh by a bastard who needed to die.

"I don't mean to make you feel guilty. I want to take care of you. To show you." He pressed a kiss right above the wound then higher up, sliding the fabric of her gown. Each touch of lips to her skin sent a jolt to her core. She wanted more kisses, and then he gently lifted her, moving the nightgown up and over her head, baring her body.

"You're beautiful," he whispered as he kneeled onto the bed, resting his head between her breasts.

She naturally reached up to stroke his hair, the short mixture of blond strands with black roots. A pang went up for him having to cut off the shoulder-length hair she'd become so familiar with. "I miss your hair."

He chuckled, the sound echoing through her body. "I miss it, too."

They lay there, her caressing him and him listening to her heartbeat.

"I'm thankful for such a sound."

"I'm grateful for any noise you make."

"No, you still don't get it. When I thought I might lose you…. I would've killed everyone there if you hadn't been breathing. I'd murder them all if they dared extinguish your light, your song."

She cringed a bit at his words, the way they filled up the aching part of her wishing for such a confession for years. To be considered important, to matter to someone. "I love you, too."

Luther's head came up then, the blue expanse of his wide eyes conveying the need for confirmation. "Do you mean it? Because my parents said they loved me, but they traded me away without another consideration. The men here, they don't love me. No, they are driven by fear, respect, and loyalty. How can you say the words? Mean them?"

"I'd ask the same of you. Trust can only be earned if a person sets aside past hurts and risks themselves again. You want me to take a chance. Can you? At this moment, I can no more prove my love for you than you can prove you'll never leave me again. But I can swear it. Pledge to be yours alone."

She meant every word, and the seconds of silence ticking by with a lack of a response flayed her open worse than the bullet wound had. Her tongue readied to take back the confession, and then Luther moved away from the bed, out of sight.

"Then I will pledge to be yours as well," he replied finally.

Eva exhaled slowly. He held up two engraving seals. One bore the image of a raven, and the other a canary. They'd used these before. When she'd spied in Hamburg, she owned a set. She used hers for writing her letters to him and vice versa. The symbol pressed into hot wax dropped on the letter, better than a signature.

"What are those for?"

He held a candle in his other hand. "To seal our pledge. Rings and jewelry can be thrown away. Words...we've been hurt by those more than healed. The symbols of us seared into the skin cannot be taken away. We will be branded to one another. Every time you see the mark, you'll be reminded of belonging to me and I to you."

With the candle lit, he held the canary to the flame first.

"Won't it hurt?"

"Love often does." The stare he speared her with caused her heart to pound. The fire in his gaze, dark and foreboding, spoke of his resolve. "I'll go first."

He set the candle into a holder on the stand next to the bed, pulled the collar of his shirt down and pressed the symbol to his chest, not far from his heart. Burnt flesh scented the air. Instead of disgusting her, it gave courage. Luther's eyes never left hers as he held the marker in place, burning his commitment to her into his skin, joining them together in a way neither of them could remove.

When he took away the silver piece, the symbol of the canary sat there bold, bright red, and scorched into his flesh. An image more beautiful than anything she'd seen.

"My turn," she said, taking the raven marker from his hand and gesturing for him to bring her the candle. She held the seal to the fire, watching closely as the metal got hot and started to burn red. The pain would serve as a rebirth and a reminder she lived. She'd let the fire wash away her guilt. "I won't be sorry anymore. I won't ask forgiveness and will believe you already bestowed it."

Parting her breasts, she inhaled as she pressed the marker to her breast bone. A growl from Luther's lips mingled with her cry of pain. It hurt like the devil but served its purpose to heal. Yet, the pain from the seal proved less than when she'd been shot. Luther sealed his hand over hers, and they both peel away the marker, revealing the raven between her breasts.

"I'm yours."

She beamed. "And I'm yours."

"Until the breath has left us. *Ti amo, dea*." I love you, goddess.

\*\*\*

The next morning, the rising sun rose at the perfect angle, casting warm sunshine on Eva's beautiful sleeping form. After their ritual branding and pledges, they'd fallen asleep, naked and covered in blankets. Her wound prevented him from taking things further, but he'd tortured them both with whispers of the sensual and outrageous things he'd do to all parts of her body once she fully healed and received the all-clear from the doctor. He'd promised to make sure every muscle, tendon, and inch of skin got exerted and properly worshiped.

In the meantime, he'd use the time until then to hunt down his prey and kill the *bastardo* who'd nearly taken everything from him.

Eva stretched and winced.

"Good morning. I have coffee."

"Au lait?"

"Is there any other way to drink it?" He smiled as she opened her eyes. She was beauty personified, her tanned skin lit up with sunlight, and his raven shone between her breasts. The skin there would need to heal as well. The burn from the canary he'd pressed to his chest lingered. The mark acted as a physical reminder of his need to avenge her near death.

Grabbing the cup of steaming coffee from the tray, he handed it over.

She sipped at the drink, sighing loudly. "What shall we do today? You could read to me, give me a bath, or feed me."

Luther laughed. She inspired such anarchy, and he'd love nothing better than to while away a day in her arms, seeing to her every need, but he'd run out of time to do such things. The new reports this morning had told him now would be the best time to strike. "Afraid I can't, my little canary. The time has come for this raven to deliver death."

"What are you talking about?" She struggled to sit up, and he moved to help her.

"Sauer. A new report has confirmed he's retreated to France and is hiding for the moment. Regrouping and trying to find a way to overcome the failure of his tunnel. This may be my only chance to strike."

"You're not planning on going alone?"

"I'll have the *Maledetto* and my crew. We'll head toward Paris in a week. I'll need to start making preparations today."

"No." She shook her head violently and set the coffee down on his nightstand. "I don't mean this ship or the crew. I mean you don't plan to go without me." The edge in her voice told him she'd fight tooth and nail, but he'd grown accustomed to delivering disappointments, especially with her.

"I won't risk another injury to you, and there's no way I'm putting you in harm's way again."

"Yet, you can do it?"

He'd never say it was because of his gender. She'd shown herself capable, in his opinion, but she could be used against him. If Sauer caught her in his crosshairs again with a gun.... He shuddered. "Yes, because I'm going to play hero for once and rid the world of someone despicable."

"You've never played hero in your life. You want to do this because you want to." She spoke the truth and read him far too quickly.

"So, what? I'm going to do everyone a favor. If I remember, we had this same argument nearly a month ago, and I'm not the one who got injured in the final fight. You did. In fact, I got damn close to killing the general, feet away, and then he fired his gun at you, his hatred for you blatantly apparent. I'd rather not give him another chance to steal you away from me." His name rested next to the definition of selfish, but he didn't care.

"Yes, but the pledge. The words, the brands. We're bonded, and I don't plan on sitting around waiting on you again. Where you go, I go."

"What about your injuries?" They'd hinder her if they got into battle.

"I'm sure you've dealt with worse. I can handle pain. The doctor said I could start moving around the middle of this week and the stitches will come out in a few days. I won't be helpless for long. Besides, you need me."

*Déjà vu.* She'd said the same things regarding the tunnel, and it had put her in danger. The risks she'd be willing to take were not worth the price she'd pay if they made a mistake. "Give me one good example of how I need you."

"I can play interference. Like Django and I did at the camp. Distractions. Pair me with him if you worry for my safety. We'll travel by ground, and you travel by air. We'll play the traders to the soldiers of his fortress."

"A trick Sauer and his men aren't likely to fall for again."

"If we disguise ourselves, they'll never know. There are many gypsy travelers wandering France and all of Europe. I believe we can do it." She went back to sipping her coffee, grown cold no doubt.

He grabbed the pot and moved to freshen her cup. "Your suggestions may have merit, but I need more details."

"The plan would be easy. We're a traveling brothel, a chance for men to cast aside their woes. We supply women, although impure, willing to do whatever. The soldiers are men. They'll fall for it."

If it worked, every man inside the compound would want a chance to entertain themselves for a few hours. "Could we time the arrival with the shift change, take out those coming on duty and irritate those who are supposed to be off duty?"

"We could arrive whenever you needed us to." Her smile brightened. "So, you'll let me go?"

"Not decided, but let's talk with Django." He considered her naked body, while running his fingertips across her breast, watching the dark nipple pebble in arousal. "*Mio inferno*." My hell.

She moaned and arched against his touch, and he couldn't help taking the tip between his thumb and index finger, rolling it between the pads and making her squirm beneath him.

"I want you, *dea*. Too much. The doctor needs to clear you for exertion soon. Until then, I'll find you some suitable clothing. I'm the only person allowed to behold you in this state." He strode off, but not before she called him a few unkind words. He prayed they'd pull this off so he'd experience her fire for many years to come.

# Chapter Twelve

The morning of departure had arrived, and Eva's entire being still revolted at the idea of Luther and the *Maledetto* heading toward Paris without her and Django's caravan to back him up. She'd asked him multiple times about Sorella and the *Liberté*. If he'd asked his sister for help or if she responded and planned to come. Each time, he either avoided the question with a kiss or told her they'd find out soon enough.

She sat in a chair in his cabin, smoking her cigarillo, and listening to Fred Astaire sing about beginner's luck, a benefit she'd never had with anything, even in love. As she blew the smoke out of her mouth, the cabin door flew open.

Her lover strode in, glowering. "You're supposed to be on the ground."

"And I wanted a good-bye kiss." She put the butt of her cigarillo out in the ashtray, and, by the time she looked up, he already stood in front of her.

"A kiss? That's all?"

She nodded. He hooked his hands under her arms and lifted her from the chair. The man carried her around with barely any effort, making her think she weighed nothing. His lips mashed into hers without tenderness or any gentle coaxing. Finally being treated like a regular person instead of someone who'd break. Their tongues danced and tango-ed as if eager to touch and then broke apart again.

When they finally stopped, she trailed a hand between their bodies and cupped his erection. "The doctor told you, didn't he?"

Luther growled. "That you're free for physical exertion, yes. But I can't take advantage of you now."

"You can't even spare thirty minutes? Even for my mouth on you."

Desire flashed in his eyes, hot and furious. He wanted her bad, and, if he would set her down, she could surely tempt him into a quick romp before he pulled anchor. As if reading her brain, he slowly lowered her to her feet, her body touching every inch of his aroused one. Maybe he enjoyed torture a bit more than the next person.

"Eva, if I could...."

"Could, an excuse if I ever heard one, but you never said no." She moved her hands to his belt buckle, freeing the leather and then unclasping his pants. Once open, she put her hands into his underwear and let the heat and hardness of him fill both palms. Her fingers started to trail downward until one rested on his balls, letting the weight further prove his need for her. "Let's get you comfortable."

Before making good on her statement, a knock sounded from over by the door. "Captain," Roscoe's voice rang out. She liked Luther's first mate, usually, except for this exact moment.

"Yes?" Luther asked, his voice a bit higher than normal as she massaged him, pumping up and down in slow, measured strokes.

"We're ready to depart on your orders, and a letter has arrived from your sister."

*Merde.* Of course, Sorella found a way to interrupt them now, not two days prior, or at sunrise. She whispered, "It can wait."

Luther chuckled. "Set her letter on the chair and shut the door behind you."

Once the door closed, he pushed his pants down, and she went to her knees. "Thirty minutes, Eva. Are you sure you want to spend them doing this? We could review the plan."

She stuck her tongue out and licked the tip of him. "We've been over everything more than twice. I'm ready."

"Yes, it appears you most certainly are."

\*\*\*

Eva waved from the ground below as the ship finally took off. Luther strode across the main deck, checking in on his men, confirming their weapons were locked and loaded, if the EMP net was fully repaired, stores fully stocked, and their course laid in.

They'd travel the Seine following it into Paris and to the *Jardin du Luxembourg*. He'd stake out the Medici palace from there, and attempt to devise the best way in. In the meantime, with his crew and technicians paving their path through the west of France, he could settle into his cabin and read the letter from his sister.

The room still smelled of sex and Eva's cigarillos. Delicious, cherry smoke things. He'd never been a fan of smoking himself, but always associated the scent with her. Picking up the letter, he settled into his chair, the afternoon sun high in the sky and his room sufficiently shaded for the moment. Her seal, the raven and fleur-de-lis, a symbol of her heritage and the marked status her husband carried, had made him chuckle the first time he'd received a letter bearing it. Now, the wax signature served as a reminder his sister was still safe. He broke the seal and began to read.

*My brother,*

*I've received your message and won't arrive in time to depart with you, but we will head in your direction. I recommend holding back. We've intercepted transmissions leading us to believe Sauer may be gathering men. You'll do well with more help, and my men are eager to spill German blood. We will meet you outside the city, near the forest of Versailles, in a week's time.*

*May your blood go unshed,*

*Captain Castoa*

He'd love to wait for his baby sister to help, but, unfortunately, time was short. If Sauer started to gather reinforcements, it'd be to his and the *Maledetto's* benefit to strike fast and hard. So forget waiting. They'd fly hot and swift, and get there as soon as possible, less than a day by his estimation, leaving them twenty-four hours to plan and then attack the following night. A faster arrival meant even less time away from Eva and the chance at keeping her out of danger Jolting out of the room, he headed for the technicians first and prayed they could stoke the tentacles of his perpetual motion engine to get them there faster.

Half a day later they'd delivered, and the *Maledetto* anchored not far from the Luxembourg Gardens. They found a building friendly toward ships settling inside the city and tied up there. They claimed to be merchants, dealing in wares. Roscoe handled the paperwork and the merchant front, so Luther took Dietrich, Hans, and two others to scout out Sauer's hideout. They grabbed bottles of wine, stopped to piss in the hedges of the garden's edge, and stumbled through the streets. Each man was assigned to take in different pieces of information—the number of entrances, the number of men guarding, and the accessibility of the garden, which proved far easier than expected.

Luther encouraged them all inside those garden walls of the hideout. They acted like drunken fools on a lark, enjoying the early summer air and a chance to see things they'd never seen, including the Medici Fountain. When the soldiers found them, they offered the men drinks—Germans being easily placated with either free offerings or with dares.

They'd explored the entire back side of the castle, and no doubt absorbed everything. Hans spoke first about leaving.

Luther followed the sentiment, rattling on about his wife. "*Merci*, soldiers. We must go home to our women. They would have our heads."

One of the Germans smiled. "You mean whores. There's no way you're married."

Dietrich piped up next, "Why would you call my wife such a name or doubt my truth?"

Gun barrels bumped up to each of their backs, and the loud, arrogant voice of General Sauer echoed behind Luther. "Because you're the same men who tried to ambush me once already, but, instead of dead, you stand here alive and well."

A small contingent of soldiers emerged, the general taking no chances this time, and Luther expected to be die. Soon. Would Sauer have the balls to do it himself? Recognition blazed in the general's eyes as he stepped in front of Luther and took the wine bottle from his hand.

Sauer sneered. "It took me a bit to figure it out, but not too long."

"I've no idea what you're talking about."

"Really, Sette? I believed your parents raised you better."

Hearing his birth name didn't affect him. At least he wouldn't let the bastard see it. "My parents never received the pleasure, since you sold me off."

"With good reason. Tell me, is she coming to help you?"

The general, with a glint in his eye, spoke of his sister, but refused to mention her. "Eva? No, she's dead."

"Your mulatto whore concerns me not at all, but lovely Sorella...she would be a prize to make up for my men's failures."

At disparaging remarks toward Eva, red flashed before his eyes. He launched toward Sauer, but a soldier smacked the back of his head with a rifle butt, and he crumpled to the ground. The general loomed over him, boot drawn back, inches from his face. "For your sake, I hope she comes. This time, she can ransom her life for yours."

\*\*\*

It took the caravan a week and a half to travel to Paris. Eva helped where she could and worked on getting her stamina back up to previous levels. She walked more often than riding in one of the gypsy wagons. Her complaints were few, outside lack of comfort and good food. The traveling troupe traded with farmers along the way. The farmers would trade food for cigarettes, so she kept her bundle of cigarillos tied to her at all times and hoarded the few she had. She allowed herself only late night or early morning drags, in fear one of the other women would see them and send a gypsy child to pilfer them in the night.

This group seemed better than other traveling caravans she'd heard of, but she refused to put all her trust in them. She spent her nights dreaming of Luther. More often than not she woke from a nightmare of him bleeding out at her feet, pleading for help. She never saw the killer, but guilt burned in her gut like the hot embers of the campfire she slept next to.

Finally, they arrived at the rendezvous point, not far from the famous French castle at Versailles. The French prime minister and his cabinet were the only ones occupying the monstrosity called a castle. Thankfully, the dense gardens surrounding the property proved a perfect place to hide and wait for the *Maledetto* to arrive. Instead of the ship, they found Roscoe. He came into camp with a small group of the ship's crew. Django received him at the wagon, and Eva moved closer. She'd never be openly involved if she didn't push for it. Django had told her Luther gave him instructions to keep her safe and out of harm's way.

*Lots of luck.* Pushing her aside under the excuse of keeping her safe seemed to be second nature to the men in her life, but she wanted to be involved. Squeezing through them, she came to the center of the circle.

"What do you mean they captured him?" Django voiced this question.

Eva's anger burst out. "How the hell did they get him? He should have met us here."

"I'd like to know the same thing." Sorella Corvino, all five-foot-four inches of her, with the braids and deerskin leather outfit, stood twirling one of her knives. She'd snuck up on the group without a sound. Eva had seen firsthand how lethal this young woman was with the small blade.

"He got your letter." The *Maledetto's* first mate nodded toward Sorella. "And Luther refused to wait.

He wanted to take advantage of potentially surprising the general before he placed all his defenses."

"Where's the *Maledetto*?" Eva asked. They'd need the ship if possible.

"Locked down. When we spied the inspectors coming, the majority of the crew abandoned ship, went into hiding. I came here with a few of the men to wait for reinforcements. Unfortunately, they expect us to come."

Eva scoffed. "A bit presumptuous. How would they have that kind of information, unless you told Sauer?" She stepped forward ready to get in his face, challenge him. Hell, Django could string Roscoe up for questioning at her hands. She'd learned how to get answers. Not all of her moonlighting work involved innocent handling of dandies or political level marks. The electo knucks in her pocket had been used to pry information from thieves in her club before.

Sorella rested a hand on Eva's shoulder. "Roscoe is my brother's most trustworthy man. He'd never betray him. They are aware we'll come to rescue my brother, and most likely they want me. Correct?"

The first mate nodded. "Yes. The general said he wants you...eh, I mean Captain Castoa. He believes she'll try to rescue Luther, and counts on it. He doesn't care if we have the same information. He believes we'll be reckless, and his contingents are in place. We've been watching, and more troops arrive every day...."

Eva took a moment to glance around at their circle.

Everyone faced the fire blazing in the middle of them. Django, Sorella, Ian, Roscoe, and the few others amassed appeared defeated and hopeless. She didn't want to give up. Giving up meant never seeing him again. "Well, then at least we have an idea of what we're up against."

Ian laughed. "There's no way I support a suicide mission. I want to live. I want my wife to live." He pulled Sorella in, pressing a kiss to the top of her head. Her halfhearted smile didn't reach her eyes.

It made no sense why they should get a happy ending and she shouldn't. Why Luther should be asked to sacrifice himself again for someone else. When would someone sacrifice for him? "Django?"

"*Ma belle*, such a plan could be risky...and I'll admit there's an appeal to staying alive."

The words inflamed her, the anger rose, threatening to explode, and she looked at Luther's sister next. "And you? Would you let him sacrifice himself for you again?"

"What are you trying to say?" Sorella frowned."

"I'm saying no one cares about the person who's given a piece of himself for everyone here, in some way, shape, or form. He saved my life, and yours. Ian would be in an American prison or labor farm if not for Luther. The entire crew found new purpose with him. Even Django's made out like a bandit between the trade materials stolen from the train and more promised."

The gypsy's eyes widened. "How did you hear about that?"

"I see and pick up more than I'll ever tell. Such talents are my business. But, now, I need to go rescue a man who's willingly given everyone a piece of himself and would do it again."

Sorella laughed. "But there's always something in it for him."

Everyone joined the petite ship captain in chuckling, nodding in agreement.

"Yes, he made his bargains. Anybody would. This world and living aren't free. People are starving. He'd starve, too, if he didn't get favors for the things he gives, payment for the items he steals. Servitude for the lives he saves."

"He saved yours," Ian piped up. "What did you give him?"

Eva removed the scarf from around her neck and undid the top three buttons to her blouse. She'd gone past the point of thinking, of caring for anything other than convincing these people, Luther's closest, the man she loved was someone worth saving. Grasping either side of her shirt she opened it and tugged down the corset top by a few inches to reveal the brand on her sternum. "I gave him my love, my pledge, to be his."

Django, Roscoe, and some of the others appeared surprised, but Sorella stepped forward and touched the mark. "This is new...and unexpected. Does he wear your mark?"

"He does."

The gypsy chimed in next. "But marks don't mean anything. Promises, vows—these are broken with the coming of new opportunities. New ideas."

Roscoe shook his head. "No, my captain doesn't make false promises. He doesn't break vows. He holds to every deal he makes, and such pacts are only broken by the other party."

More murmurings through the small group of consensus, confirming the first mate's words and their own experiences with Luther.

"He could be dead already," Django said right before he tossed back the rest of whatever booze he'd been drinking. Probably some wine they'd gotten in the last town. "Then the trip would be worth nothing."

"If it gives us a shot at taking out the general, then Luther would say it's worth it." *Damn.* She never imagined she'd fight this hard to keep him alive, after the years she'd spent wishing him dead. Conversation resumed, even Ian and Sorella whispered between each other. The talking didn't produce results, though, and they needed a decision before dawn.

Eva walked into the center of the group near the fire. The flames warmed her in the chilly, night air. Silence fell, making her faith waiver. Without her lover, the continued fight against Germany would take a serious hit. He represented so much more than a man who did things for people for a price. "So, where do we stand?"

# Chapter Thirteen

The rattle of the wagon wheels had its own cadence, a rattle and a clank like the beginnings of some blues song she'd sung before, all about hell hounds and chasing devils. That's what they were doing, tempting fate in the name of a possible useless rescue. Eva chose to focus on the positives. Luther had to be alive, bait for Sorella. The possibility they'd take down over a dozen German soldiers who stood for something, though some may be conscripted like Henri. Mere boys and young men promised a handful of things, including food, and sent off to train to kill and murder in the name of a ruler they'd never meet.

*Damn.* Her mind had wandered back to those poor souls. Yet, she couldn't ask Django to not allow the women, all dolled up to put on a show, to protect themselves with the knives, and electo weapons hidden on their persons. Her knucks were tucked into the pockets on her skirt, ready to be deployed. The only problem, no one possessed guns. A new favorite. Gunpowder didn't get shorted by an EMP.

"Are you ready? We're almost at the gate." Django whispered his words, tugging on the brim of his cap. He played driver to her lady-in-charge.

"Just let me do the talking. I've run a cathouse before."

The command came just then. "*Halt. Was ist das?*" What is this?

Eva let her German come forth. It hadn't been easy to learn, but she'd forced herself so she'd understand her enemy always. "Entertainment. For the men? Everyone needs a little time to unwind, and there's no company, at least female, in the big drafty house up the way. If there's one thing my girls can do, warming men up tops the list. And at no charge.... After all, you're here to protect us." She batted her eyes then, leaning over from her perch so they got a good flash of breasts. "*Nein?*"

The one on her left got the first glimpse. He moved from his position at the entrance to the gatehouse and smiled wide, teeth far from perfect and a crooked nose broken at least once. "Geoff, they want to entertain us."

"I'm not interested in girls like her," Geoff replied a lip curled.

Eva whistled and snapped her fingers behind her. "Marie, come out here."

In less than a minute, the only blond gypsy she'd ever met came out of the back of the wagon, circling until she stood at Eva's feet. Marie twirled a lock of hair between two fingers, dangling her other hand over her breasts. These women knew how to entice.

Geoff and Crooked Nose stood in thrall.

"I understand you have particular tastes, and Marie here follows direction really well. She only likes to keep good company. If you want, I can leave her here with you both—if you promise to share and radio up to the house so we don't get shot at going up the drive. These girls in here, they are all lonely. All the good men get taken away to the army."

"*Frau*, it's no problem. I'll radio right now. Geoff, keep Marie company." Crooked Nose stepped into the booth and grabbed a phone, dialing a number. He muttered a few words into the mouthpiece, doing his best to keep his voice under control, but the mere idea of sitting pretty with a willing female had him acting a little screwy. He slammed the phone down and sauntered back to Eva, winking at his companion, who'd already started kissing Marie. "You're clear to go on up. After I check the wagon for weapons."

Eva shrugged. "Do what you must."

Django nudged her, but she refused to respond. The materials they hid wouldn't easily be found. No, these fools would search in a hurry so they could claim their prize. Sure enough, Karl failed to disentangle himself from Marie, and his partner merely flipped the cover on the back of the wagon. When the girls catcalled at him, the search ended.

The soldier tapped the back of the wagon twice. "You're ready to go, and we'll take care of Marie until you come back."

Django flicked the reins, and the horses picked up the trot again. "I'll deploy the girls and start the party—"

"I'll slip off into the house and around the back to meet Sorella, Roscoe, Bastille, and Ian."

"Do you really think there won't be other soldiers guarding the back?"

"If there are, I can take care of them, but I doubt it." Men deprived of female flesh could be pretty predictable. The moment ladies arrived, the desperate fellows started thinking with anything but their heads. The only one she'd never seen such a tactic work on was Sauer. "These men haven't sunk themselves into anything in months, possibly a year or more. We're bringing them a wagon full of women eager for a ride or multiple ones. They will line up to get a chance."

Sure enough, when they brought the wagon to a halt in the main courtyard, a small crowd of soldiers had gathered, all in uniform, with their weapons nowhere in sight. These men appeared desperate, if their hungry eyes and lopsided grins were any indication.

"*Bonjour*, my little soldiers. I'm Madam Canari, and in this wagon are a dozen ladies anxious to make your acquaintance. These women are to be treated kindly, and, in return, they will treat you well." She winked at few of the men up front. Stepping down slowly onto the stones below, she smiled big and drew them in. "They only ask for a fire. For the night air can get chilly, even with your warm bodies."

The soldiers scrambled then, gathering wood, forming a small bonfire in the center of the courtyard. They didn't care about Eva as she slipped around them and entered the house. The other women had already disembarked from the wagon and assisted the men with the fire, being useful and accommodating. *All according to plan.*

Once through the front doors, she made her way to the back of the house. A few lamps illuminated the house, though the entire thing could easily be ablaze thanks to Tesla's technology. She kept her steps damn near silent and moved along on tiptoe, not letting the heel of her boots touch the tile. She'd opted for pants tonight rather than a skirt. The men would be less likely to be interested, though her color would ensure additional disinterest, which also worked in her favor.

She took her time opening the back door and slipping out to check for any additional guards. So far, smooth sailing, and when she jogged down the steps of the terrace, she nearly ran face first into the lone guard on duty.

"*Frau? Wo gehst du hin?*" Where are you going?

"I'm searching for you. The others are gathering in the courtyard. They said you kept watch out here all alone without any company." Eva stretched a hand up to stroke the soldier's cheek, the rough bristles of his facial hair abrasive against her fingertips.

Behind the soldier, there was movement. Shadows advancing in the dark, and she made sure to keep her quarry occupied.

"Have you been stationed here long?"

"Only a few weeks."

She smiled at him. "How long since you've had a woman?"

Clouds parted and the moonlight shone down at that moment, revealing Sorella and Bastille moving toward them. A few more seconds and they'd be close enough to put this one on the ground.

The soldier took her question as an invitation and pulled her close, abandoning his hold on the pulse gun in his hands and slinging it around his body to his back. "Long enough. I'll take any woman willing to give me a moment."

Definitely a mood killer. She apparently held little appeal to him, but the dip just wanted a quick screw. Before she could utter a reply, the soldier grunted in pain then leaned toward her. She backed up as his body dropped to the ground. "I'm not as desperate as you are."

Sorella stepped up, wiping her blade on her pant leg. "Where are the others?"

"All in the courtyard as planned."

When Sorella glanced down at the man she'd just killed, Eva followed up with, "Most of them. There may be a few still on duty like this one. So they wouldn't be in trouble for completely abandoning their posts."

Ian and Bastille each grabbed two of the dead soldier's limbs and hoisted the body into some bushes off to the side.

The trained assassin nodded then did what she did best...took over. "All right. You will search the upstairs with Ian. Bastille and I will take the main floor, kitchens, and any cellars. Luther's somewhere. We'll find him."

"Wait a minute. I think you and I should pair together and send the boys to take care of the ground floor and cellar. We're most likely to run across Sauer on the top level, and I don't want to stumble into him with only Ian for protection." Eva side-eyed Ian, unwilling to pretend she'd trust him to keep her safe. "No offense."

"None taken. I don't trust you all too much either. You betrayed Luther once. I'm okay with my wife accompanying you. If you prove untrustworthy, she can take care of you quickly." The bastard didn't mince words. He never had, and he seemed committed to the idea of killing her if she planned to betray them.

"But you hated Luther."

"He's my brother-in-law, and I've warmed up to him for the most part. He fights the good fight now. He's not a saint, but neither am I." Ian winked at her then pulled his wife in close for a kiss. "Hurry back to me."

Inside the house and two flights of stairs later, they made the perfect pair—assassin and singer—searching rooms as silently as possible. About halfway down the hall, a male scream resounded, and the anxious ball in her stomach dipped lower, like a sinking stone. Silent running was a skill, and Sorella did a better job of it than Eva, but she tried her hardest to keep her boots from slamming on the marble floors. Ridiculous concept, fancy floors. She'd keep thinking about stupid things like interior design instead of the possibility the scream belonged to Luther.

Down the corridor, the screams got a bit louder, and when they finally found the room producing the sounds, Eva didn't want to see beyond the closed door. The ornate gold designs on the cream coloring gave an illusion of something marvelous, but, once they pushed the barrier open, the opposite would be true.

Sorella motioned to her, pointing a finger at Eva's waist, then imitating sliding something onto each hand. Eva pulled her knucks out, slid them into place, and fired them up. Her partner drew two knives and took the lead, her skill with a blade far superior than Eva's with the knucks.

A flip of the handle and a shove sent both double doors flying inward. Sorella charged into the room, arms bent at the elbow and knives poised to throw. Time halted at the vision of Luther, stripped to his underwear, strapped to bedposts, a soldier slapping him with an electo cat-o'-nine-tails. A vicious little weapon she hadn't seen in years. Blood ran freely across his back, arms, and legs.

The soldier stared at them, pure hate and surprise etched onto his face. Sorella yelled, "*Bastardo!*" Too bad the word came as she threw her knife, with the second balisong following the first in rapid succession, providing no reaction time. The torturer fell to the floor, and Eva walked into the room. Another German scum dashed out from behind the door, halting her advancement. Eva's vision went red at a chance to get back at the enemy, and her fists flew. She hollered a battle cry, pummeling the idiot's chest then his face when he fell to his knees from the force of the electric volts hitting his body. No one would take someone else she loved away from her, no one.

She finally stopped when the sound of Sorella calling her name broke through her rage. "Eva? Canary, you can stop now. He's dead."

Eva slowly stood, a bit drained but waiting for the guilt, the shame at taking a life to wash over her. It didn't. No feelings came, except relief she'd protected someone she loved. *Luther*. She rushed to his side to assist Sorella who'd already cut the ropes holding him hostage.

"Is he breathing?" She reached out to touch his arm, trembling as she came in contact with his blood-matted arm hair.

"Quit talking about me when I can hear you fine. What are you doing here?"

"Rescuing you." Eva lifted his arm and pressed a kiss to the back of his hand. He didn't wince, a good sign.

"I never asked you to. In fact, I told you if things went wrong to stay away."

Sorella scoffed. "Stop being an ass, Brother. You should thank her for convincing the rest of us to come and get you. Can you stand?"

"Prop me up, and I'll make it happen."


Luther used Eva and Sorella like crutches but did his best to keep the majority of his weight off them. They had enough of a burden to deal with. Reality came to him slow, hazy. There was something important to say, but every bone ached, and he couldn't summon the words. Every muscle burned with each step and movement his body made.

Getting out of the room proved easier than he expected, but he slowed them down. In the hallway, Sorella suggested what he'd already considered. "Let's put him down on this bench, and I'll check the stairs."

The elegant seat creaked under his weight. He leaned his head back against the wall, trying to form coherent thoughts, to get the words out. "General. Silent alarm trigger."

Eva crouched in front of him and took his hands in hers. Always so soft, she'd never stop being soft on him. But her words belied the misunderstanding, the verbal mistakes he made. "We've already taken care of the guards. They're in the courtyard. We can't find the general. Where is he?"

"There are more guards." He forced the words out, and alarm dawned on her face, her eyes going wide.

"Sorella," she called out.

His sister had already disappeared down the hall around a corner and the sound of boots, like a small herd of cattle on the march, echoed around them. Eva stood, dropping her connection with him. She turned her knucks back on, and the electricity buzzed in the night. If they only had these weapons, they'd be dead soon enough.

"Eva, I'm sorry," he muttered, hanging his head. He'd failed to protect her.

"Quit talking nonsense. You've got nothing to be sorry for. If anything, I'm sorry we didn't find you any clothes."

He laughed then, and doubled over in pain. "I failed, and you worry about clothes."

The thundering herd of soldiers grew louder. Unintelligible shouts sounded through the corridor, and his sister spouted German back at the fools. It wouldn't be long before weapons fire would occur. His sister had less of a chance of defusing this situation than she had of finding him clothes in this monstrous house.

"You're funny when you barely make sense," Eva replied as the coil guns rang out. Buzzing bolts of electricity zinged down the hall and hit the walls.

Within minutes, Sorella came running around the corner, then a door opened at the opposite end of the hallway and soldiers burst out and raced toward them. Eva threw a few punches, and he tried to stand. Getting up proved a struggle he was willing to make. He'd die protecting the woman he loved. Once he finally gained purchase with his feet, though leaning against the wall, Eva screamed. Sorella came to a stop next to him, throwing two balisongs through the air. Both hit the guards flanking Sauer, who held Luther's woman captive, a knife to her throat. His sister had already taken out the other soldiers. Gunfire exchange continued behind them, as the soldiers yelled at some unseen force on the approach.

"*Frau* Sorella, how kind of you to join us. Your brother must be happy to see you, too."

His sister spat on the floor in front of them.

The general sneered. "Being among savages has turned you into one. No worries. Once you're among civilized society, you'll be back to your usual self."

"She's never going back," Eva replied, struggling against him and nicking her throat in the process.

Luther held one hand out. "Stop moving, sweetheart."

"Yes." Sauer pushed the knife against her wound, opening it wider. "Or this will go a lot faster, mulatto whore. I want to tell you what I did. I burned your precious club to the ground and the people there, the ones we left alive, scattered."

Luther growled. With every word, the *bastardo* all but proved how twisted and insane he'd become. "Why?"

Her lover asked the very question she wanted to, but she couldn't form the words through the wave of grief cascading over her body. For so long, she'd held onto the misguided idea she was doing everything for them. For the promise they'd all be free together. The things she told herself were so very different from the lies Sauer had used to keep her under his thumb.

Before she could take action, he started talking again. "I did it because every last one of them reflected the filthy scourge in our land. Mixing the races, Jews, gypsies, blacks, Spanish…none of you are pure. Not like these boys dead beside me or the thousands of soldiers fighting for the kaiser. I'll purge this continent one whorehouse at a time and she"—he jerked Eva upright against him and repositioned the knife—"a mixed race bastard slut who sleeps around and sings about her dirty heritage as if living the way she does is something to be proud of, will be made an example of. She'll come with me. Luther, you'll die, and Sorella will return and fulfill her obligation to the man who invested millions of coin in supporting her education."

The idiot's monologue gave her time. The time needed to slip her hand into her pants pocket and retrieve the necklace from her mentor. She waited as patiently as one could with a knife at her throat and disgusting diatribe being spouted next to her ear.

Luther said something else, but she couldn't hear the words and lost any hope of concentrating on anything besides the chance to get the upper hand. Her senses became tuned to Sauer's stance, the position of his arms around her, and how tightly he held her. With the right counter move, she'd be free and able to get away.

The press of the knife loosened, and Sauer's voice went soft. "To want a better world for the children of Germany is not unrealistic. To want a civilized world."

Eva ducked her head, tucking her chin against her wet, bloody neck, and pivoted her hip to throw the general's balance off. They swayed, and his arms fell away, swinging in the air in a natural attempt to find equilibrium. She avoided the wild, waving hand with the knife and turned to face him.

Opening the locket, she stepped forward as he finally righted himself. "You won't be getting your civilized world, nor my lover or his sister. You'll get what you deserve." Lips pursed she blew across the top of the locket and sent a fine white powder into the air.

Sauer coughed and then laughed. "You're quite the backwater bitch thinking face powder would—"

The knife clattered to the wood. The general's words were replaced with screams and howls of agony as he clawed at his face. He slumped to the floor, face purple from lack of oxygen, and his cries of anguish turned to gurgles from a man who'd be dead in minutes.

Sorella and Luther stood at her back by the time he stopped breathing, with Luther resting a hand on her shoulder. "What did you have in there?"

"I'm not sure, and I never asked, but I once watched a woman drop a man bigger than you to the ground with it, and it took five of us to drag his dead body from the bordello. Mademoiselle killed him for raping her...she left me a bottle of this stuff, and I've kept this little bit with me."

Luther laughed. "Why did you wait to use it?"

"I'm not going to kill someone without a backup plan." She leaned into his touch, refusing to be miffed about his humor in her reserve. Better to be happy he lived.

"No, but you're braver than most." Sorella bent over the dead men and retrieved her balisongs. She wiped them against her pant legs. "I'd have never worn a poison I didn't know the name of or the effects. Lucky we're not all dead."

Eva pulled back, sure the risk had been there, but... "Better dead than in a madman's clutches."

"Agreed, my little canary." Luther hugged her then leaned into her with a groan.

Ian and Bastille came around the corner, a few guards dead near their feet. Ian announced the best news she'd received all day, "The soldiers are all taken care of, and we're free to leave. Providing everyone can weave around all the dead bodies."

"Let's get us all out of here," Eva said, supporting her man and eager to leave the fanciful building behind.

# Chapter Fourteen

*One month later....*

Luther had never believed in marriage, at least not the kind with true love, forever and always stuff. Until now. Seeing Eva walk toward him, without an escort, in a cream confection of lace and beads had him thinking of their wedding night as much as the years to come.

His sister leaned down from her perch on the step above him to whisper in his ear, "Funny how you get a fancy ceremony and I got some piss poor marriage in my captain's cabin."

"She deserves the best after what she went through. After I left her."

Sorella chuckled. "Whatever you say, Brother."

The bride reached his side, and Luther wrapped his big hand around her small, soft one. Since the escape, he'd spent most of his time putting his crew to work on rebuilding her club, after buying the land himself. She couldn't own property, but he could, and he'd be damned if she didn't get things back the way she had them.

He pledged to restore her club, as long as he could use it as a safe house for those fighting the good fight and needing a place to hide. Though the details remained hazy, they'd agreed on the most important points. When they didn't agree...the sex afterward smoothed the rough edges.

Eva smiled up at him as Sorella gave the opening remarks. He tuned her out, focusing instead on his beautiful bride. The glow about her had recently sprung up, like an ethereal glow from a Tesla lamp. More words, the exchange of vows, and he said a few I dos and I promise. Then his sister told him he could kiss his bride.

Taking the new Mrs. Corvino in his arms, he pressed his lips against hers. The spark between them hotter than ever, and he dipped his tongue into her mouth, savoring the moment. Plenty of cheers and whistles rang out from the seats, some from his Maledetto crew, including Roscoe, Sorella, and Ian, and Django's unruly band of gypsies.

Hours later, the cheers continued with every dance, toast, and reason they could think of. He hadn't been this happy in years nor seen such happiness, with the exception of the day he'd married his sister to Ian.

Funny how thinking of the pair brought them to his side.

"How does it feel to have a ball and chain?" Ian's question ended with a grunt as Sorella jabbed him in the ribs.

"I'm not a ball or a chain. I'm a finely tuned weapon who can kill you if you make me angry." She smiled, but the words held a note of a promise.

Luther chuckled. "It feels marvelous. Honestly, I'm waiting for the right time to sneak my bride off so we can be alone. I'm tired of everyone as well."

Django patted his shoulder, and Luther nearly threw a punch at him. "Ha! I practically snuck up on you. How can you be tired of us? We throw the best parties."

"Yes, and eat the most food. And drink the most wine," Luther replied with a wink. To be honest, he'd never tire of happy celebrations. But reality would soon stop them. "Did you see the latest papers?"

Luther, Ian, Sorella, and Django all nodded. The main story reminded him work would need to begin again and soon. How long before Germany was in a place to continue its conquering ways? "The story has been confirmed and the engagement announced. The son of the United States president will marry a French princess. There will be an official party and courtship in Paris."

Sorella growled. "I always knew the kaiser had kept more of us but didn't honestly believe they'd treat us like we're interchangeable."

"The way of the kaiser," Django said with a sad smile. "He believes us to all be pawns for him, with no cares or consideration for how we each have our own brains...our own feelings. Luther, you say you want someone on the inside for this party?"

"I'll need someone, yes. I want ears, eyes, and a person in place in case an attempt is made on the president or his son."

"Then I volunteer. Young love so nice, *non*?" The gypsy left their small group then, strolling back to wrap his arms around another woman and take her onto the dance floor. Something in the way he'd talked told Luther there was more to his reason for volunteering, but having someone not clearly associated with his group would be easier to implant. After the last few months, Django had proven his loyalty in spades. Paying the man didn't hurt Luther either.

"What is everyone doing over here being all serious and quiet? We are celebrating my wedding. We should be happy." Eva pushed between Ian and Sorella and wrapped herself around him. He was blessed.

"Is there anything else you want, my wife?"

"Oh, I like you calling me wife better than little canary." True, his new name for her fit. "And I want you and me upstairs in ten minutes."

Luther laughed, pulling her in for a quick kiss. "So she has decreed, my brother and sister. My wife requires my immediate attention. Till tomorrow."

The pair nodded and started to move away, with Eva pushing them on, "Yes, go dance. Make merry. Put off business until tomorrow...afternoon."

"Afternoon?" He started with her toward the entrance to her club. The building officially opened in a few weeks. In the meantime, they had the whole upstairs, including her fancy new room, to themselves.

"Yes, I have big plans."

\*\*\*

Hours later, with the sun setting in the west, Eva stepped onto the terrace and looked out at her friends and family still celebrating below, though they'd started several fires as daylight had begun to disappear.

"Would you like a cigarillo?" Luther said from behind her.

She pulled her robe tight, the satin soothing her heated skin. His arms came around her, a lit cigarillo in his hands. Eva shook her head. There'd be no smoking for a while, not now. "I'm afraid I can't, makes my stomach upset."

"Very strange, I've never heard my wife to turn down tobacco."

"Well, your wife has never been pregnant either."

The cigarillo fell from his hand and hit the terrace mortar, sending sparks a couple inches in every direction. He swallowed hard and then asked, "You're going to have a baby?"

Turning to face him, she caught the shocked expression and the joy in his eyes. "Yes."

He picked her up, kissing her the whole way. Pulling back, after plundering her mouth thoroughly, he grinned. "I'll have an heir. We'll have a child."

Eva had never seen him so happy, and as they watched the sun dip below the horizon, she eagerly anticipated tomorrow and whatever new adventure their future held.

# Sign up for the Decadent Publishing Newsletter here

# Prologue

*New Orleans*
*1936*

Gretchen pulled the scratchy half-blanket tight around her shoulders and took a step closer to the fire, a small orange blaze inside a busted metal pot. What little heat came out warmed her bare legs, her threadbare cotton dress barely coming past her knees. She didn't have long, mere minutes, before mother noticed her gone, snuck off to hear the storyteller again. Except he wasn't on the small stool set against the wall like normal. If he didn't appear soon, she'd have to leave.

"Please," she whispered, her breath visible in the chilled night air blowing in from the coast.

The answer to her plea—a cat's loud howl. Startled, she looked away from the fire.

"Come for a tale, little one?" He squatted onto the stool, no taller than her. He'd a long beard, gray and grizzled, like the tangles of wires her older brother tried to straighten. His voice was scratchy; her mother said it happened because the storyteller loved to puff on the steel pipe he kept in his jacket pocket.

"Yes, Nicodemus." She loved his stories, the tales he'd share. It didn't matter if they were real or not; they gave her something to think about besides being tired or hungry.

"Then gather close. Warm yourself by the fire, wee one. For a gift, I'll tell you one of my favorites."

Searching, Gretchen looked all around, down at the ground, over her shoulder. What could she give, for she had nothing? Then she leaned in and pecked a kiss on his wrinkly cheek.

He smiled. "Thank you. You'll need a special tale for such a special gift." He stroked his beard, eyes focused on the flames licking the air in front of them. "Once upon a time, there lived a girl born to parents who'd prayed for a daughter but never expected one."

"Was she special?"

Nicodemus tapped her hand with two fingers. "So special a band of thieves kidnapped her when she was a tiny thing, not much younger than you are. Her parents had no choice but to trade her brother in exchange for her safe return. The girl's future would crown her the queen of a kingdom upon her wedding day. With black hair, pale skin, and eyes as deep blue as the Mediterranean Sea, she'd be Europe's true jewel."

"I've never been to the Meditearret...Med..: the sea."

"Why would you? It's thousands of miles away, and you have the Gulf right at your fingertips. You have no doubt seen the water that washed along those shores, for it travels long distances over time, more so than people." He chuckled. "Now, do you want to hear the rest?"

"Yes." She blushed. Even her mother said she always spoke too soon, no hesitation.

"The would-be princess didn't want her throne and ran away, searching for her lost brother and hoping to rescue him like he had saved her all those years ago."

Gretchen put her hand to her chest, trying to rub out the ache the story put there. To care about someone so much, to be cared for—

"Greta-girl!" Her mother's high-pitched yell echoed down the alleyway.

She ignored the call and looked back at Nicodemus, who puffed on his pipe, curls of smoke wafting into the air. Tugging on his coat sleeve, she asked, "Where is the princess?"

Before he uttered a reply, a hand clasped around her arm and yanked. With her free hand, her mother cuffed the back of her head. "I've been looking everywhere for you. Left your brother to do your work for you? We'll see how you like not eating then."

Gretchen rubbed her eyes to keep the tears from flowing.

Mother spat on the ground at Nicodemus's feet. "Stories." The word sounded like something cursed. "A bunch of drivel and a waste of time. Back to work, girl."

The words came with a shove to Gretchen's back, and she nearly fell, face first, as she took those few stumbling steps forward. Somehow she managed to stay upright and start the trek back to the busy main roads. The roads where her mother searched for a buyer, where she'd have to worry about being sold, and where no would save her.